Ambush of the Mountain Man

Also by William W. Johnstone
in Large Print:

Blood of the Mountain Man
Code of the Mountain Man
Courage of the Mountain Man
Pursuit of the Mountain Man
Valor of the Mountain Man
War of the Mountain Man
Cunning of the Mountain Man
Fury of the Mountain Man
Rage of the Mountain Man
The First Mountain Man: Preacher
The Last Gunfighter: Imposter
The Last Gunfighter: Rescue
Quest of the Mountain Man

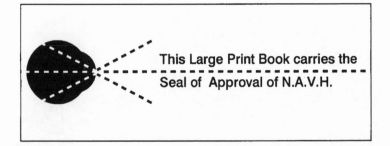

This Large Print Book carries the
Seal of Approval of N.A.V.H.

AMBUSH OF THE MOUNTAIN MAN

WILLIAM W. JOHNSTONE

Thorndike Press • Waterville, Maine

Published in 2004 by arrangement with Kensington Books, an imprint of Kensington Publishing Corp.

Thorndike Press® Large Print Western.

The tree indicium is a trademark of Thorndike Press.

The text of this Large Print edition is unabridged.
Other aspects of the book may vary from the original edition.

Set in 16 pt. Plantin by Minnie B. Raven.

Printed in the United States on permanent paper.

Library of Congress Cataloging-in-Publication Data

Johnstone, William W.
    Ambush of the mountain man / William W. Johnstone.
      p. cm.
    ISBN 0-7862-6469-1 (lg. print : hc : alk. paper)
    1. Jensen, Smoke (Fictitious character) — Fiction.
  2. Rocky Mountains — Fiction. 3. Mountain life —
Fiction. 4. Large type books. I. Title.
PS3560.O415A83 2004
  813'.54—dc22   2004047998

AMBUSH OF THE
MOUNTAIN MAN

National Association for Visually Handicapped
serving the partially seeing

As the Founder/CEO of NAVH, the only national health agency solely devoted to those who, although not totally blind, have an eye disease which could lead to serious visual impairment, I am pleased to recognize Thorndike Press* as one of the leading publishers in the large print field.

Founded in 1954 in San Francisco to prepare large print textbooks for partially seeing children, NAVH became the pioneer and standard setting agency in the preparation of large type.

Today, those publishers who meet our standards carry the prestigious "Seal of Approval" indicating high quality large print. We are delighted that Thorndike Press is one of the publishers whose titles meet these standards. We are also pleased to recognize the significant contribution Thorndike Press is making in this important and growing field.

Lorraine H. Marchi, L.H.D.
Founder/CEO
NAVH

* Thorndike Press encompasses the following imprints: Thorndike, Wheeler, Walker and Large Print Press.

One

Smoke Jensen and his friends, Cal, Pearlie, and Louis Longmont, turned their horses' heads south and rode out of the town of Noyes, Minnesota. They rode slumped in their saddles, dog-tired after the months they'd spent in Canada working for William Cornelius Van Horne.

Cal, still excited about the adventures they'd had and the unforgettable scenery of the northern Rocky Mountains, jabbered on and on about how he wished he'd been born in the days of the mountain men.

Louis and Smoke just looked at each other and smiled, for they knew those days hadn't been nearly as romantic as they'd sounded in the stories Cal had heard around the campfire from Bear Tooth and Red Bingham and Bobcat Bill.

Of course, they weren't about to tell the young'un that and ruin his ideas about the "good old days."

They rode on for about two miles, until they came to the railroad station that was their goal.

As they reined in their mounts in front of the stationmaster's office, Louis stretched and observed, "That was very nice of Bill Van Horne to arrange for us to ride all the way back to Big Rock on the train instead of on horseback."

"Yeah, it'll sure save some wear an' tear on my backside," Pearlie agreed as he stepped down out of his stirrups. "The way I feel now, if'n I never see another saddle as long as I live it'll be all right with me," he added, rubbing his butt with both hands.

Smoke laughed. "Not only that, but Bill said we could ride in James Hill's own private car on our trip south."

"Hill?" Cal asked. "Ain't he the man Bill said bought up all the railroads in this part of the country?"

Smoke nodded. "That's right, Cal. Hill owns just about every inch of railroad track between here and home."

"Jiminy, then his own private car ought'a be somethin' to see."

"I would imagine it will be rather lavish," Louis said as he got down off his horse.

"I don't know what lavish means," Pearlie said, "but I hope it means it's stocked right well with food, 'cause I'm hungry enough to eat a bear."

"Well, now, that's a surprise," Cal said sarcastically to his friend. "From the way you was talkin', I figured you'd be too tired to eat an' you'd just go right to sleep once we got to the train."

Pearlie looked at the young man as if he'd uttered a blasphemy. "What? Go to sleep without eating? What kind of man would do that?"

After Smoke spoke to the stationmaster, and their horses and gear were stowed in the cattle car, the man showed them into James Hill's private car. As they entered, he told them to just pull the bell rope next to the door if they needed anything and a steward would take care of it.

Just before he left, he stopped in the door and looked around the car, shaking his head. "You boys must be powerful friends of Mr. Hill's," he said, " 'cause this is the first time I've ever seen him loan his car out to anyone." He paused and grinned. "Hell, when the President came out here last year on a tour, Mr. Hill gave him another car. Said this one was too good for politicians to use."

"Thanks for all your help," Smoke said, smiling and shutting the door behind the man.

As the stationmaster stepped down out

of the car, a man moved out of the shadows next to the station building and stood there staring at the train.

When the stationmaster approached him, the man ducked his head and put a lucifer to the cigarette dangling from the corner of his mouth. He looked up, tipping smoke from his nostrils, and gave the stationmaster a lopsided grin. "Howdy," he said in a friendly tone of voice.

"Hello," the stationmaster answered. "If you're here to buy a ticket on this train, you need to see the man in the ticket booth inside the building."

"Thanks," the stranger answered. "I might just do that." He turned toward the building, hesitated, and then he looked back over his shoulder at the stationmaster.

"Uh, by the way, was that man I just saw getting on the train named Smoke Jensen?"

The stationmaster nodded absentmindedly, already thinking about the dozens of things he had to see to before the train could leave the station.

The stranger cut his eyes back at the train before he went into the station to buy a ticket. His eyes were filled with hate.

When he got to the ticket booth, he

10

pulled a wad of cash from his vest pocket and placed it on the counter.

"Can I help you, sir?" the ticket man asked.

"Yeah. Can you tell me how far Smoke Jensen and his friends are going?"

The ticket salesman looked down at an open book in front of him and pursed his lips for a moment. "I believe they're ticketed all the way through to Big Rock, Colorado," he said, glancing back up at the man standing in front of his window.

"Then give me a ticket to the same place," the man said, pushing his money under the gated window.

"Yes, sir."

"And I need to know if I have time to send a wire before the train leaves."

The ticket man pulled a watch from his vest pocket and shook his head as he looked at it. "No, sir, I don't believe you do."

"Damn," he muttered.

"But I'd be happy to send one for you after the train leaves if you wish."

When the man nodded, looking relieved, the ticket man pushed a piece of paper and a pencil under the window gate. "Just write out who you want me to send it to and what you want to say and I'll get it on over to the telegraph office just as soon as the train leaves the station."

"Uh," the man stammered, his face burning scarlet. "I can't write too good."

The ticket man pulled the paper back and smiled. "Then just tell me what you want to say in your message and I'll write it for you."

"It's to Angus MacDougal in Pueblo, Colorado." The man thought for a moment and then he said, "Just say our friend is headed for home . . . should be there in ten days."

"Will there be anything else, sir?" the ticket man asked as he folded up the paper.

The man grinned through thin lips. "No, I think that ought'a 'bout do it."

After Smoke closed the door and turned around, he saw Louis pouring himself a glass of brandy into a bell-shaped crystal goblet from Hill's private bar in the corner. Louis swirled the amber liquid for a moment, and then he sniffed delicately of the aroma. His face relaxed and he smiled, as if he had died and gone to heaven.

Cal had taken his boots off and was lying back on the overstuffed sofa, poking the cushions with his hands, feeling how soft they were.

Pearlie was over in the opposite corner and he had his hands on the bell rope, about to pull it.

Smoke cleared his throat loudly. "Pearlie, what are you doing?"

Pearlie glanced over at him, his face blushing slightly and looking embarrassed. "Uh . . . I'm just ringing this here bell to see if the man who answers it can get us some food 'fore I faint from hunger."

Smoke shook his head, pointing to the corner of the car where a coffeepot was steaming on a fat-bellied stove. "Why don't you have a cup of coffee to fill your gut until the train leaves the station? Then we can see about getting some grub."

"Coffee?" Pearlie asked, as if he'd been offered something horrible to eat.

Louis looked up from where he stood at the bar. "And Pearlie, there's a bowl of sugar and a pitcher of cream here on the bar to sweeten it up with."

Pearlie grinned halfheartedly and moved toward the potbellied stove. "Well, now," he said amiably. "I guess now that you mention it that coffee will do for a start."

"Coffee does sound good," Cal said, getting up from his perch on the couch. "But Louis, you'd better dole that sugar out to Pearlie a little at a time if'n you want any

13

left for the rest of us to use," he added as he followed Pearlie toward the stove.

"You sayin' I'm a sugar hog, boy?" Pearlie asked, poking Cal in the shoulder with his fist.

"No, not exactly," Cal answered, rubbing his shoulder and frowning. "It's just that sometimes you like to put a little coffee in your sugar."

Two hours later, the men had finished their meal and were sitting around a table in Hill's private car getting a poker lesson from Louis. Luckily for Cal and Pearlie, they were playing for pennies instead of dollars, because Louis and Smoke were each winning just about every hand.

Just as Louis was leaning over to rake in another pot, the train suddenly slowed, its steel wheels screeching as the engineer applied the brakes with full force.

"What the . . ." Louis began to say when the chips and cards all started to slide across the table from the sudden slowing of the train. Cal moved his head to the side toward the nearby window and called out, "Looky there!" and pointed off to the side of the train.

A group of men could be seen suddenly appearing from a copse of trees near the

14

track, all riding bent down low over their saddle horns, guns in their hands and bandanna masks over their faces.

"Well, I'll be hanged," Smoke said, his lips curling into a slight grin of anticipation. "It looks like the train is going to be robbed."

Louis unconsciously reached up and patted the wallet in his coat breast pocket, thick with the money Cornelius Van Horne had paid them for helping with the surveying for his Canadian Pacific Railroad the past six months. "I'll be damned if any two-bit train robbers are going to take any of my money!" he exclaimed.

Smoke pulled a Colt pistol from his holster and flicked open the cylinder, checking to see that it was fully loaded. "No one's gonna take any money from any of us, Louis," he promised, the grin slowly fading from his face.

"I'll get our rifles from our gear in the next car," Pearlie said, referring to the sleeping car next door where they'd stored their valises and saddlebags.

"Bring some extra ammunition too," Smoke said, glancing out of the window. "It looks like there're fifteen or twenty riders out there we're gonna have to contend with."

He ducked down out of sight, motioning the others to do the same, as the train slowed and the group of riders drew abreast of the car they were in.

A gunshot rang out and the window next to Smoke's head shattered, sending slivers of glass cascading down onto his back and causing a tiny, solitary drop of blood to appear on his neck. He reached up and wiped it with his finger. "First blood to them," he said in a low, dangerous voice.

The train continued its rapid deceleration. Probably because the robbers had dynamited or obstructed the tracks in some manner, Smoke thought as Pearlie came scuttling back into the car with his arms full of long guns. Smoke took the Henry repeating rifle from Pearlie, and watched as Louis took the ten-gauge sawed-off express gun and an extra box of shells from him.

"You're gonna have to get awfully close for that to do much damage," Smoke said.

Louis grinned. "I thought I'd wait until they came knocking on our door and then give them a rather loud greeting," he said in a light tone of voice that was belied by the dark fury in his eyes.

Smoke nodded. "Good idea. I think I'll take Cal and Pearlie and slip out the far side of the car when the train stops. When the bandits get off their horses to make their way through the cars, it'll give us a chance to scatter their mounts."

Pearlie nodded, grinning. "And then they'll be trapped out here in the middle of nowhere with nothing to ride off on. Good idea, Smoke."

When the train finally ground to a complete stop, Louis turned a big easy chair around until it was facing the door, and then took a seat, the express gun across his knees and his pistols on a small table next to the chair. He pulled a long black cigar out of his coat pocket and lit it, sending clouds of fragrant blue smoke into the air. He pulled his hat down tight on his head and leaned back, crossing his legs and smoking as if he were waiting for a friend to visit.

"Good hunting, gentlemen," he called as he eared back the twin hammers on the shotgun.

"You be careful, you hear?" Smoke said, tipping his head at his friend.

"It is not I that should be careful, pal," Louis replied, his voice turning hard. "It is those miscreants that are interrupting our trip who should be saying their prayers at this time."

As Smoke and the boys slipped out of the car and moved slowly down the line of cars toward the front of the train, Cal asked in a low voice, "Smoke, what's a miscreant?"

Smoke chuckled. "It's someone without a shred of decency in their character, Cal."

"Oh," Cal said, glancing at Pearlie walking next to him. "You mean like someone who'd take the last spoonful of sugar in the bowl and not leave any for his friends?"

"Now Cal, boy," Pearlie said in a soothing voice, "that there bowl wasn't near half-full to begin with."

As they neared the car just behind the engine that contained wood to be burned in the boiler, Smoke heard a harsh voice say, "Watch the hosses, Johnny. We'll get the passengers' money and be right back."

Smoke gave the robbers time to climb aboard the train before he put the Henry in his left hand, sauntered out from between two cars, and walked slowly toward the outlaws' horses, which were being tended by a large, fat man with a full beard and a ragged, sweat-stained hat set low on his head.

The outlaw's eyes widened and his hand

moved toward his belt as he said, "Who the hell . . . ?"

Smoke drew his Colt in one lightning fast motion and shot the man in the face, blowing him backward off his horse to land facedown in the dirt next to the track, his gun still in its leather.

The other horses jumped and crow-hopped at the sound of the pistol shot until Cal and Pearlie untied them from where they had been hitched to the rail on the railroad car and shooed them away by waving their arms and shouting.

Soon, only the dead outlaw was left next to the tracks, blood still oozing into a puddle under his head.

Smoke moved up to the engine and found the engineer lying on his side, holding his left arm, a bullet hole in his left shoulder.

Smoke knelt next to him. "Are you gonna be all right?"

The engineer nodded. "Yeah, but somebody needs to put some wood in the boiler or we're gonna lose all our steam."

Smoke glanced over his shoulder. "Cal, would you help this man and do what he says while Pearlie and I go after the robbers?"

"Aw shucks, Smoke," Cal groused as he

climbed up into the cab of the engine. "Pearlie gets to have all the fun."

"We just don't want you getting yourself shot again an' bleedin' all over Mr. Hill's fine car," Pearlie teased, "you bein' such a magnet for lead an' all."

"Now Pearlie," Cal argued, his face turning red. "I ain't been shot in over three weeks now."

Smoke laughed. "That might be because we haven't been in any gunfights for three weeks, Cal."

Cal bent and helped the engineer to his feet as Pearlie and Smoke jumped down out of the engine and headed back along the tracks toward the passenger cars.

They eased up into the first one, and Smoke was surprised when a female passenger threw up her hands and screamed, "Oh, no, they've come back to rape and kill us!"

Smoke smiled and motioned for her to put her hands down. "No, ma'am. We're here after the robbers," he explained as he and Pearlie moved down the aisle between the seats.

She took one look at Smoke's handsome face and broad shoulders and her voice seemed a mite disappointed when she said, "Then you aren't going to rob the men

20

and rape the women?"

"Not this time," Smoke called back over his shoulder with a grin.

Smoke and Pearlie moved through three more cars before catching up to the robbers in the car just before Hill's private one that Louis was in.

Smoke motioned for Pearlie to kneel down in front of the door, and then stood over him as he jerked the door open.

The crowd of robbers in the aisle collecting passengers' money and jewels glanced back over their shoulders in time to see Smoke and Pearlie open fire, Smoke working the lever of the Henry so fast his shots seemed to be one long explosion.

Six outlaws went down before the others could return fire, and then it was wild and poorly aimed as they shouted and screamed and backed through the far door of the car, which was so filled with gunsmoke they could barely be seen.

The bandits in the lead jerked the door to Hill's car open and rushed inside, to be met by the thundering explosion of twin ten-gauge barrels hurling buckshot at them.

Four more men went down, shredded and almost cut in half by the horrendous power of the express gun.

The seven men remaining alive dove off the train out of the connecting door to the cars, and began running as fast as they could back up the tracks to where they thought their horses were tied.

They slowed and looked around with puzzled expressions when they came to Johnny's dead body.

"Where the hell are the hosses?" one of the men hollered, whirling around and looking in all directions.

From thirty feet behind him, Smoke said, "They're gone, you bastards!"

The robbers turned and saw Smoke and Pearlie and Louis standing there, side by side, their hands full of iron.

"There's only three of them, boys, let's take 'em!" one of the men shouted.

"Uh-uh," came a voice from behind the outlaws. Cal stood there just outside the engine, his Colt in his hand. "There's four of us," he said, a wide grin of fierce anticipation on his young face.

Nevertheless, the outlaws swung their pistols up and opened fire.

In less than fifteen seconds it was all over and every gunman lay either dead or dying next to the train. Blood pooled and saturated the dry earth of the tracks.

Smoke and Pearlie and Louis approached the group of bodies on the ground cautiously, kicking pistols and rifles out of reach of the wounded men who were groaning and writhing on the ground.

Cal said softly, "Dagnabit!" as he glanced down at his thigh, noting a thin line of red where a bullet had creased his upper leg, burning rather than tearing a hole in his trousers.

He quickly turned to the side so his friends couldn't see the wound, calling, "I'm just gonna go on up and make sure the engineer is all right."

When the engineer looked at the blood staining Cal's pants leg, Cal shook his head. "Don't say nothin' 'bout this to my friends, all right?"

The wounded engineer just grinned, having heard what Pearlie and Smoke had said about Cal being a magnet for lead. "I promise not to say nothin', if you'll be so kind as to build me a cigarette while we wait for the steam to build."

Two

Carl Jacoby sat staring out of the train window next to his seat, sweat beading on his forehead and running down his cheeks as he thought about just how fast with a gun Smoke Jensen and his friends had proved to be.

Jacoby was one of Johnny MacDougal's best friends . . . or at least he had been until Jensen and his men had shot his friend down in the streets of Pueblo, Colorado, last year. Jacoby hadn't been there, being sick with the grippe at the time, but he'd been told Jensen had shot Johnny down in cold blood without even giving him a chance to clear leather.

Being also hopelessly in love with Johnny's older sister, Sarah, Jacoby had at once told the family he would do anything they wanted to help them get even for Johnny's untimely death. He'd hoped this would endear him to Sarah, but she hadn't seemed to notice him when he made the offer just after her brother's funeral. She'd been quiet and kind of off in her own world, as if she was thinking of something else.

Old Angus MacDougal, eaten up with grief and the need for vengeance, had questioned Sheriff Wally Tupper about where Jensen and his friends had been heading after they'd killed his son. Sheriff Tupper had said that one of the men, a Cornelius Van Horne, was a famous Canadian railroad builder.

Angus had done some checking, and afterward he'd sent Carl up to Canada to follow Jensen and his men and to let the old man know when they headed back to the States so he could avenge his son's death.

He'd told Jacoby to stay out of Jensen's way, not to brace him or to let him know he was being watched, but just to keep an eye on him and make sure they didn't leave Canada without Jacoby knowing about it.

Jacoby had done so gladly, sure that no one could have bested Johnny in a fair fight, him being the quickest man with a short gun Carl had ever seen — that is, until the gunfight he'd just now witnessed.

He was watching out the window as Jensen and the three men with him went up against outlaws who outnumbered them two to one. He'd gasped in disbelief when he'd seen the cowboys blow the out-riders off their feet without even breaking a sweat.

Hell, he thought, sleeving sweat off his forehead, I was watching Jensen when he drew and I still didn't see his hand move it was so fast, and the gents with him were just a hair slower, if that.

He didn't think the outlaws would've gotten a single shot off if they hadn't already had their guns in their hands, and still they hadn't managed to draw blood from Jensen or any of his friends.

Jacoby shook his head, remembering how many times he'd been tempted over the past six months to just step up to Jensen and draw his gun and shoot the bastard. His stomach grew queasy at the thought of what would have happened had he been so foolish — he'd be lying dead and buried in the godforsaken wilderness above the border, that's what. He snorted. Hell, as fast as Jensen is and as slow as I am, he'd have had time to build and light himself a cigarette and still could've shot me deader'n yesterday's news.

He turned his head from the sight of the men from the train picking up the dead outlaws' bodies and stacking them in an empty boxcar, and thought about what he was going to do next. He knew that if he continued on his mission for Angus MacDougal, sooner or later he would have to go up against Jensen and his friends, and that thought scared him half to death.

On the other hand, if he quit now and headed back to Pueblo with his tail between his legs, he was sure Sarah MacDougal would never give him another look — at least not the kind of look he'd want her to give him. She'd more than likely think him a coward and a fool, and would never again give him the time of day.

Damn Johnny to hell, he thought angrily. If he'd just kept his mouth shut and hadn't tried to play the big man like usual, I wouldn't be in this mess.

Jacoby looked up as the conductor came down the aisle, telling all the passengers that they would be on their way shortly and that all of their money and valuables would be returned to them at the next stop, thanks to Smoke Jensen and his friends.

"Uh, sir," Jacoby asked, raising his hand like a schoolkid to get the conductor's attention.

"Yes, sir?" he asked, stopping next to Carl's seat.

"Will there be a telegraph at the next stop?" Carl asked, almost hoping the man would say no.

"Why, yes, I believe there is, sir."

"Thanks," Carl replied, turning his mind to just what he was going to say to Angus. He knew he'd better warn him about Jensen's ability with a gun, but he didn't want to come off sounding like he was afraid of the man, even though the plain truth of the matter was he was more frightened of Jensen than of anything else he could imagine. Carl scrunched down in his seat and pulled his hat down over his eyes. This was going to take some heavy thinking before they got to the next stop if he was going to get it right.

After all, he remembered, Angus MacDougal don't exactly take kindly to being told he is wrong about anything, and especially not about this.

Angus MacDougal sat on his porch smoking a corncob pipe, still wearing his black mourning suit even though it'd been more than six months since his only son had been shot down in the streets of Pueblo, Colorado.

He glanced up from his reverie at the sound of hoofbeats rapidly approaching his ranch house. He nodded slowly to himself when he recognized the portly figure of Sheriff Wally Tupper riding toward him. Must be some news from Carl, he thought, getting slowly to his feet and stretching to get the kinks out. He felt like he'd aged ten years since Johnny died, but then the death of a loved one will tend to do that to a person, he reasoned as he walked down the porch and waved a greeting at the sheriff.

Tupper climbed down out of the saddle and held up an envelope in his hand as he climbed the steps to the porch. "Got this here wire for you from Carl Jacoby, Angus," he said, his voice deferential as if he worked for Angus instead of the town of Pueblo. "It came in on the telegraph just this mornin' and I rode right out here to bring it to you first thing," Tupper said.

Angus took the paper, his eyebrows knitting together over a scowling face. "What's it say?" he asked.

"I dunno," the sheriff replied, his face screwing up in fright. "I wouldn't presume to read a wire addressed to you, Angus. You know that."

Angus smiled a halfsmile, reveling in the look of fear and trepidation on the sheriff's face. He couldn't help it, he just loved to intimidate other men, especially men who were supposed to be in authority.

"I know you'd better not, Wally," he said in a low, hard voice. "Now go on into the kitchen and have the cook fix you some coffee while I read this, and then we'll talk."

Angus slit the envelope with a thumbnail and pulled out the folded sheet of paper. It was indeed a telegram from Carl Jacoby. Angus squinted his eyes — it looked to be from some pissant town in Minnesota that he'd never heard of before. Sighing at the indignities old age put on him, Angus reached into the breast pocket of his coat and pulled out a pair of reading spectacles he'd taken to using in the last year when he found he was unable to read the local newspaper without holding it way out at arm's length.

The telegram read:

HAVE SEEN JENSEN AND HIS MEN IN ACTION STOP VERY IMPRESSIVE STOP DO NOT THINK THEY WOULD HAVE TO BACKSHOOT ANYONE STOP PLEASE CHECK SITUATION AGAIN BEFORE PROCEEDING STOP SHOULD ARRIVE BIG ROCK SEVEN TO TEN DAYS DEPENDING ON WEATHER END

CARL

Angus crumpled up the paper and gritted his teeth so hard his jaw creaked. He whirled around and stomped across the porch and into his house. He found Sheriff Tupper drinking coffee out of a mug and flirting with his Mexican housekeeper, Lupe.

Angus took a deep breath and tried to calm down as Lupe poured him a cup of coffee and put it on the table in front of him.

"Would you excuse us, Lupe?" he asked, struggling to keep his voice soft. "Man talk."

"Certainly, Señor," she said, and quickly vanished from the dining room.

Tupper raised his eyebrows when he saw the crumpled sheet of paper in Angus's hand. "Bad news?" he asked over the rim of his cup.

Angus didn't answer until he'd gotten to his feet and walked over to the cabinet against the wall. He opened the door, took out a bottle of whiskey, and poured a dollop into his coffee, pointedly not offering any to Tupper.

"Tell me again about the day my boy Johnny was shot down, Wally," Angus ordered shortly as he took a sip of his whiskey and coffee.

"You sure you want to hear all that again?" Tupper asked, his face showing his discomfort. The day he'd brought Johnny's body home to Angus, he'd thought for a moment the old man was going to kill *him,* as if *he'd* done something wrong.

"I asked, didn't I?" Angus responded angrily, slamming his cup down so hard the coffee sloshed over the rim.

"Well," Tupper began quickly, trying to picture that day in his mind, "from what I heard from those who were there, Johnny and the boys had been drinking a mite, an' they proceeded to tease Jensen and the men with him about how they smelled. Shortly, one of those old mountain men riding with Jensen jumped up and . . . uh . . ." Tupper hesitated, trying to decide how graphic to get with his description of the events. Finally, he decided to be a bit vague. "Jumped up and knocked Johnny to the floor."

"And Johnny hadn't drawn on the man up till then?" Angus asked, his eyes full of sorrow and anger.

"Nope," Tupper replied. "Matter of fact, Johnny was flat on his back after the man attacked him without no warning," he said, shading the truth a mite because he knew that was what the old man wanted to hear.

"What happened then?"

"Well, sir, Johnny's friends took him outside an' they waited for Jensen and his men to come out of the Feedbag an' into the street."

"And when they did?"

"This is where the stories all get a mite different," Tupper said. "Johnny and his friends all had their guns in their hands when I got there, but only Johnny's had been fired, an' he'd only gotten off the one shot. But the man with Jensen, a William Cornelius Van Horne, said Johnny and his men had fired at them first an' started the fracas."

Angus drained his cup, his face pale at hearing once again how his boy had died. "And you believed him, even though none of the boys managed to get a shot off?"

"I didn't have no choice, Angus. This Van Horne man carries a lot of weight in the state, an' he knows the governor personally."

"And tell me again, just how many times was my boy shot?" Angus asked.

"Uh, the undertaker said he had over six slugs in him, Angus."

"And you honestly think, knowing how fast Johnny was with a six-gun, that he could be standing there with his guns out

33

and only get off one shot whilst someone else has to take the time to draw and ends up shooting him six times?" Angus asked, his voice incredulous. He shook his head. "No, sir! There ain't nobody alive that fast," he finished without waiting for an answer.

"Well, what do you think happened then?" Sheriff Tupper asked.

"I think those bastards shot my boy and his friends down in cold blood, and then they took out their guns and put them in their hands so it'd look like a fair fight," Angus said, his voice tight with anger.

Before Sheriff Tupper could answer saying there'd been plenty of other witnesses to dispute Angus's version of the gunplay, the door opened and a pretty young woman in her mid-twenties walked into the room, her face a mask of anguish. It was obvious she'd been listening to Tupper and Angus from the other room.

"That's not all they did to him, Daddy," Sarah MacDougal said through jaws tight with anger.

Angus cut his eyes to her. "What do you mean by that, Sarah?" he asked.

"Sarah, do you really think this is necessary?" Sheriff Tupper began, a worried look on his face.

"Yes, Wally, I do!" she answered. "My father deserves to know the truth about what was done to his son and my little brother."

Angus slammed his fist down on the table, causing the coffee cups to leap into the air and spill dark liquid all over the wood.

"Damn it!" he shouted. "Don't talk about me like I wasn't even in the room!" He turned his gaze to the sheriff. "Wally, if you know more than you've been telling me for the past six months, you'd better spit it out now or I'll make you wish to hell you had."

Tupper reached out and turned his coffee cup back right-side-up, clearing his voice. "Well, Angus, when I got to Johnny's body, I saw a deep cut on his cheek and saw that his two front teeth had been knocked out."

"What?" Angus shouted, half-rising to his feet.

Tupper held out his hand, palm out. "Now hold on, Angus. I asked around and it seems Johnny was raggin' the men with Jensen 'bout them being smelly and dirty, an' one of the old mountain men took offense at it and pulled out his Colt and pistol-whipped Johnny with it." Tupper took a deep breath. "I didn't say nothing about it 'cause it was plain to see that Johnny had picked the fight in the first place."

Angus sat back down, slowly nodding his head. "Now I see why Johnny was waiting outside for those men to leave the saloon. His pride was hurt because of the beating he took in front of his friends."

Sarah stepped over and laid her hand gently on Angus's shoulder. "That doesn't alter the fact that Johnny was shot down in cold blood, Daddy, and that was after they slashed his face and knocked his teeth out."

Angus turned sad eyes to his daughter and covered her hand with his. "You're right, Sarah. Even though Johnny was spoiled and a hothead who never knew when to shut his mouth, he didn't deserve to be shot down in the street like a stray dog for it, him and his friends both."

Tupper leaned forward, his arms on the table. "Now Angus, don't go off half-cocked. Johnny's dead, and there ain't nothing you can do gonna change that." He took out his handkerchief and wiped his sweaty forehead with it as he continued. "Killing Jensen and his men won't change anything, Angus."

Angus looked over at the sheriff and his lips curled in a deadly smile. "No, I can't change it, Wally, but I can sure as hell make sure someone pays for what they did to my boy."

Sarah blinked back tears, and turned and walked slowly from the room and out the door to stand on the front porch, staring at the mountain peaks in the distance. She'd always hated Johnny, ever since they were little kids. Up until she was five years old, she'd been the apple of her daddy's eye and he'd taken her everywhere with him, teaching her to ride and shoot like a man.

Then, Johnny had been born and her life had changed forever. All of a sudden, it was as if she ceased to exist and her daddy's world revolved around his new son.

It hadn't been fair; from the beginning, she could ride and shoot better than Johnny, and was smarter in the bargain. But that didn't matter to Angus MacDougal. All he cared about was having a son to carry on his name. Well, that was over now, Sarah thought bitterly. His precious son's big mouth had finally gotten him into some trouble their daddy couldn't buy his way out of.

Sarah shook her head and entered the house again, and walked into her room and began to pack her bags. She planned to be in Big Rock when Smoke Jensen and his friends arrived. She had it all worked out in her mind: She'd move into town using a fake name, get a job, and no one would know she'd come there to put Smoke Jensen in his grave.

As she flung her clothes into the valise, she thought that maybe then Angus would again give her the respect and attention she deserved.

Three

Sheriff Monte Carson was waiting at the station in Big Rock when Smoke Jensen and his friends, Cal, Pearlie, and Louis Longmont, got off the train.

The four men looked tired and their faces were drawn from the long train ride from up near the Canadian border, and it looked as if they'd all lost weight on their journey to Canada and back.

As they stepped down out of the passenger car, Monte turned to his deputy. "Jim, why don't you see to their horses and luggage and I'll take them over to Longmont's Saloon." He chuckled. "They look like they could do with some good food for a change."

Monte walked over and slapped Smoke on the shoulder, smiling at the men standing next to him. "Well, boys, I'll bet it's good to get home, ain't it?" he asked.

"It is certainly good to get my posterior off of those torture devices the railroad calls seats," Louis said, stretching and rubbing his butt at the same time. "I do believe they stuff those seats with rocks," he added, wincing at the pain in his buttocks.

"Just think how bad it would'a been if we would'a had to sit in regular seats 'stead of those padded ones in Mr. Hill's car," Pearlie said.

"I'd rather not think about that eventuality, if you don't mind," a grouchy Louis rejoined.

Monte's deputy tipped his hat and said hi to the men before he walked off down the platform toward the baggage and livestock cars.

"Jim's gonna get your hosses and luggage and all," Monte said. "Why don't we head on over to Louis's place and get some good grub into you boys," he said, hesitating before adding, "you all look like you been starved half to death up there in the North Country."

Pearlie's tired face broke into a wide smile. "Did I hear somebody say grub?"

Smoke nodded. "That sounds awfully good, Monte. I could use some coffee that I don't have to chew before swallowing." He smiled. "After riding with mountain men for a spell, any coffee that won't float a horseshoe is considered too weak to bother with."

"Yeah," Cal added. "Like they said, their

coffee don't take near as much water as you think it do," he said, doing a fair imitation of Bear Tooth's growl.

Daniel Macklin sat on a bench at the far end of the platform, whittling on a stick and watching the men as they moved off toward the downtown area. He'd been on this same bench watching the arrival of each and every train that'd pulled into Big Rock for the past three months. His lips curled into a slow grin as he realized his job was just about over.

The fingers of Macklin's right hand twitched as they hung just above the butt of his pistol, tied down low on his right thigh. He forced the hand to relax, deciding to wait until he'd contacted Angus MacDougal before he braced Jensen. He hoped when Angus found out Jensen was back in town that he would wire him back giving him permission to kill the son of a bitch. That would be fitting, he thought, since the men Jensen had killed had been some of his best friends.

He got slowly to his feet, dropped the sharpened stick to the ground as he leaned his shoulder against the corner of the building, and waited for Carl Jacoby to get off the train. Angus had wired him Jacoby was trailing Jensen, so Macklin figured he'd be somewhere on the same train.

Sure enough, a few minutes after Jensen and his friends had left, Macklin saw Jacoby exit a car further down the track. As Jacoby put his bag down and looked around, Macklin gave a low whistle and grinned. Jacoby was also a good friend of his, though Macklin thought he was a dumb ass for mooning over Sarah MacDougal like a hound dog in heat. Sarah would never give ordinary cowhands like them the time of day — she had been groomed since she was just a pup for finer things, men more important than country boys. Of course, that was before her brother had been killed. Who knew what was going on in her mind at this stage?

Jacoby nodded, picked up his bag, and walked toward Macklin. "Hey, Mac, how're you doin'?" Jacoby asked.

Macklin looked down at the large pile of wood shavings from his whittling and grinned. "I'm doin' a mite better now that you and Jensen are here," he replied, glancing over his shoulder at Jensen's group as they walked down the street away from the station. "I'm sick of coolin' my heels here for the past few months waitin' on y'all to get back from the North Country."

"I hear that," Jacoby said, nodding his agreement. "Come on," he added, "show me to the nearest saloon. My mouth's so dry I'm spittin' cotton."

Macklin pursed his lips and narrowed his eyes. "Don't you think we'd better wire ol' Angus first and tell him everbody's here?"

"Naw," Jacoby said, waving his hand in dismissal of the thought. "I wired him from along the way tellin' him when we were gonna get here. Besides, there's some things I gotta tell you 'fore we decide on just how to proceed with this matter, important things."

Upon hearing that his boss and friend was back, Andre rushed from the kitchen in Longmont's Saloon and wrapped his arms around Louis's shoulders, giving him a quick kiss on both cheeks in the French manner.

"Thank you, Andre," Louis said, smiling at the man who'd been both his chef and his good friend for many years. "I'm glad to see you also."

"But Monsieur Louis," Andre said, clucking his tongue and shaking his head as he stepped back and took a good look at Louis. "You have lost much weight on your journey. Did not those railroad men up there in Canada feed you?"

"Not nearly enough, Andre," Pearlie piped up from the rear of the group of men.

Andre glanced up and smiled. "Ah, Monsieur Pearlie, my most ardent customer."

"If ardent means hungry," Pearlie said, "you sure got that right, Andre." He took his seat at the table and stared at the chef with anticipation. "How long before we can get some lunch?"

Andre laughed. "I will get to work immediately," he said. "I will see that fresh coffee is prepared while I fix you a lunch that will put some weight back on your bones and some strength back in your muscles."

The men all took seats at Louis's regular table just as the young black man who was the head waiter appeared carrying a tray with a silver coffee service and five mugs on it.

As they drank their coffee, Monte leaned back and said, "All right now, boys, tell me all about your adventures up there north of the border."

"First, Monte," Smoke said, "I want to know if you've heard from Sally."

"Oh, dagnabit, I almost forgot," Monte said. "I got a wire yesterday that said she'd gotten your telegram saying you were on your way home. She said her father is doing much better and she will probably be here in the next week or so."

Smoke didn't answer, but the smile on his face showed he was pleased at the news. Before he'd left for Canada a few months back, his wife Sally had gone back East to be with her ailing father. Smoke was glad to hear the man was better and that she'd be home soon, for he missed her terribly.

Pearlie stuck a cigarette he'd built into his mouth, leaned back as he got it going, and proceeded to give a slightly exaggerated account of the men's adventures in the Canadian wilds over the past six months. He ended his narrative with the tale of the train robbers. "And Cal here actually got into the gunfight with us without getting wounded, if you can believe that!" Pearlie said, taking a breath and finally getting around to sampling his coffee, which was cooling by now.

Cal unconsciously reached under the table and rubbed the sore spot on his thigh where he had in fact been slightly wounded, something he'd managed to keep from his friends. It wasn't his fault that bullets just naturally seemed to seek him out, no matter how careful he was in the gunfights. Luckily, though he was a frequent target, none of the wounds had been overly serious.

Monte laughed and slapped Cal on the back. "Well, now, that is something. Maybe your luck's changing, Cal," he said just as Andre appeared followed by two waiters with platters of heaping food in their hands.

Pearlie hurriedly stubbed out his cigarette and rubbed his hands together. "All right!"

Andre caught Louis and Smoke's eyes and winked. "I am glad to see that you are so hungry, Monsieur Pearlie," he said, nodding his head.

"I'm so hungry I could eat a horse, Andre," Pearlie said, straining in his chair trying to look and see what the platters held.

"That is good, my friend, for I have just acquired a new supply of frog legs and escargot from my supplier in Denver this very morning."

Pearlie made a face and sat back in his chair. "Uh, Andre, no offense, but I think I'll just skip the frog legs and try some of that es-car-go, or whatever it is. It shore smells good, I'll tell you that."

"And I assure you, Monsieur, it will be a taste you will never forget, especially when you dip the little creatures in the melted butter I've made."

"Uh . . . did you say somethin' 'bout little creatures, Andre, or did I misunderstand?" Pearlie asked, his face suddenly showing signs of suspicion.

"*Mais oui,* Pearlie, I did say creatures."

"But, Andre. Just what are es-car-go?"

"Snails, my friend, large, plump, juicy snails," Andre replied.

Pearlie put his hand over his mouth and started to get up from the table until he saw what was on the platter the waiter was setting down.

He grinned and pointed. "That looks like beefsteak to me, Andre."

Everyone at the table laughed, even Pearlie, and they all grabbed knives and forks and dug in.

Four

Macklin took Jacoby by his hotel, arranged for him to get a room there and dropped off his luggage, and then showed him to a restaurant that served both liquor and food.

While they drank a glass of whiskey and waited for their food orders to arrive, Jacoby told Macklin about the gunfight on the train between Jensen and his friends and the outlaws who'd outnumbered them.

Jacoby shook his head and drained his glass, sleeving whiskey off his lips with his arm. "It was the damnedest thing I ever seen, Mac," he said, his eyes wide with wonder. "One minute Jensen an' his friends are standing there in front of maybe ten outlaws, an' 'fore you could spit, they hands was full of iron and they was blasting the shit outta those hombres."

"Just because a man's an outlaw don't necessarily mean he's fast on the draw, Carl."

"That's just it, Mac. All of them bandits already had their guns in their hands when Jensen and his men drew down on 'em."

"And you're sayin' none of those outlaws managed to draw any blood?"

Jacoby held his glass up and pointed at it so the waiter would bring him another. "That's just what I'm saying, Mac. Jensen and his men walked away from that fracas clean as a whistle. And what was even more funny is they didn't wait for the bandits to make a play at them or try to take their money. They went looking for the outlaws as if they kind'a enjoyed the thought of a good fight."

Macklin's eyes narrowed as he stared at Jacoby. "Just what are you sayin', Carl? You sayin' Jensen is faster on the draw than Johnny MacDougal was?" he asked, his face showing his doubt that such could be the case.

"Hey, Mac, I'm telling you the truth," Jacoby insisted. "I know Johnny was fast with a six-killer 'cause I've drawed against him in contests before, but Jensen is faster, by a long shot!"

Macklin stroked his jaw as he let his eyes drop to stare into his whiskey. "So, you think it may've been a fair fight when Jensen shot Johnny down in Pueblo?" he asked, keeping his voice low so the nearby diners wouldn't hear him mention Jensen's name.

Jacoby shrugged. "Hell, I weren't there, Mac, so's I can't say for certain. All I know is Jensen could snatch a quarter off'n a rattler's head and leave two dimes an' a nickel in change 'fore the snake could strike." He raised his hand to the waiter and indicated he wanted another drink and he wanted it fast. All this talk about how fast Jensen was with a gun was making him nervous. Sweat formed on his forehead when he remembered how he'd once planned on bracing Jensen himself.

After the waiter placed two more glasses on the table in front of them, Jacoby glanced down at the way Macklin was wearing his gun low on his right hip. "And by the way, Mac," he said, pausing to take a deep draught of his drink, "I've seen you draw before too. So if you're planning on going up against Jensen, you'd better plan on shooting him in the back from a long way off, or I'll be taking your dead body back to Pueblo with me when I leave this burg."

Macklin's face flushed and he gritted his teeth for a sharp retort, but was interrupted by the waiter reappearing with a platter containing their food orders on it in his hands. When the waiter left, Jacoby, who'd noticed the angry expression on

Macklin's face when he warned him not to try and outdraw Jensen, wisely decided to change the subject before Macklin got really pissed off.

He cut his steak and stuck a piece in his mouth, asking around it, "You been here long enough to ask around, so what is Jensen's reputation in his town?"

Macklin busied himself with cutting his own steak and didn't look up at the question, though he snorted derisively through his nose. "Hell, around here they think he's better than homemade apple pie," he answered. "I couldn't find a single person in this entire town had a bad word to say about Jensen or the men riding with him." He stuck the meat in his mouth and added, "Hell, seems Jensen himself founded this town some years ago, so naturally nobody's gonna say nothing against him."

Jacoby sighed. "That's what I was figured you'd say," he said as he used his fork to rake some corn onto his knife and then stuffed it into his mouth. "From what I seen on the train, Jensen is pretty much a square shooter," he added as he chewed thoughtfully.

Macklin shrugged and asked, "So what? Angus MacDougal didn't send us here to check out his character. He sent us here to let him know when he got home an' possibly to put a bullet in him and his friends."

"But Mac," Jacoby said, shoving his plate to the side and leaning forward, "what if his fight with Johnny was fair an' it was like they said, that Johnny fired off shots at them first? Hell, we all know what an asshole Johnny could be when he was all liquored up."

"Don't make no never mind to me what happened back in Pueblo," Macklin answered, his eyes burning. "All I know is Johnny and the others that died with him were friends of mine, an' I aim to see Jensen in his grave for what he done to them!" He paused for a moment, staring at Jacoby as if he were an enemy instead of one of his oldest friends. "An' I aim to do it with you or without you, Carl, so don't be getting in my way or you're liable to catch some lead too."

Jacoby snarled back, "Don't go playin' the big man with me, Mac. Remember, I seen you draw before an' I ain't all that certain you could take me, even if you was crazy enough to try."

"Well, then, how 'bout I put it like this. Old Man MacDougal been pretty good to both of us, it seems, so if'n he wants Jensen dead, for whatever reason, it's plenty good enough for me."

Jacoby started to reply, but Macklin added, "And what do you think Sarah is gonna say when she hears you've gone all soft and sweet on Jensen, the man what killed her baby brother?"

Jacoby let his eyes drop to what remained of his meal, his appetite squashed by the question. "Maybe if I explain to her that —"

"Explain what?" Macklin burst out. "That the man who put six slugs in her little brother after bashing out his front teeth is really a nice feller and we should just forget about the whole thing?"

Jacoby leaned his head back and rubbed the back of his neck with his hand, trying to ease the sudden pain there that Macklin was causing. "You're right, Mac, she'll never understand," he said wearily. "She's like her father. She don't never forget a slight, and she sure as hell won't care what I think about Jensen's character, that's for sure."

"If you're finished with that steak, maybe we'd better get on over to the telegraph office and wire Angus and see what he wants us to do," Macklin said, stuffing the last piece of his meat into his mouth, thinking Jacoby was a fool for caring so much about a lady that would never ever give him the time of day.

Sally Jensen eased out of her seat on the train when it pulled into the station at Pueblo, Colorado. The next stop would be Big Rock, and she wanted to freshen up a little before arriving home. She hadn't seen Smoke for more than half a year, and she wanted to look her best when he met her at the station. She could already imagine him throwing his arms around her and squeezing her tight against his hard body.

When she looked into the mirror in the women's parlor compartment as she applied a light dusting of powder and just a hint of lip rouge, she noticed that the thought of seeing her man again after so long was making her cheeks flush and burn as if they were on fire.

She grinned, speaking at her image in the looking glass. "Why, Sally Jensen, you're acting like a hussy instead of an old married woman!"

"Pardon me?" a young woman who was just entering the compartment asked, raising her eyebrows at the sight of Sally talking to herself in the mirror.

Sally laughed, her cheeks flushing even more at being seen acting so strangely. "Oh, don't mind me, miss," she said, waving a hand at the young girl. "I'm just returning home after a long absence, and the excitement of seeing my husband and home again after so long has me behaving a bit silly."

The young woman stepped in front of another mirror across the room and spent a few moments adjusting her hat and dress. Sally thought the girl probably wasn't used to wearing such nice clothes, the way she picked at the buttons and continually fussed with the ruffled collar on the neckline. And she certainly didn't know how to wear a frilly hat. She had it at completely the wrong angle.

"Here, let me help you with that," Sally said, moving over to smooth out the ruffles in the back of the dress and make it a bit more comfortable for the young woman and to adjust the tilt of the hat to a more rakish angle.

"Thank you," the girl said, smiling. She stuck out her hand. "I'm Sarah . . . uh . . . Sarah Johnson," Sarah MacDougal said, stammering a bit over the false name she'd decided to use on her trip to Big Rock to see what she could do about making

Smoke Jensen pay for what he'd done to her little brother.

"Hello, Sarah," Sally said, taking her hand and shaking it. "I'm Sally Jensen."

Sarah flushed when she heard Sally's last name, and ducked her head as she tried to think of something to say. She'd had no idea the man might be married, and to such a refined-looking woman as Sally obviously was. If she'd thought about it at all, she would've thought a gunman like Smoke Jensen would probably be keeping company with a dance-hall gal or one of the fallen doves in a house of ill repute somewhere.

Sally, seeing the girl's discomfort but not knowing what was behind it, asked, "Are you traveling far, Sarah?"

"Uh . . . just to Big Rock, Mrs. Jensen," Sarah answered in a hoarse voice with just a trace of a tremor in it.

"Oh, just call me Sally, Sarah," Sally said, smiling and returning to her own mirror for a last-minute adjustment. "We're not very formal in Big Rock, as you'll find out when we get there."

"All right, Sally," Sarah said, bending to pick up her valise.

Sally put her arm through Sarah's as they left the compartment. "Why don't you sit with me, dear, and you can tell me all about your trip to Big Rock," she said, leading Sarah to her row of seats.

After Sarah had stashed her valise on the overhead rack, she sat down next to Sally and they began to talk.

"Are you visiting friends or family in Big Rock?" Sally asked, wondering to herself what would make a young woman set out all alone on such a trip.

"Uh, not really, Sally," Sarah answered. "I just had to get out of Pueblo, and Big Rock seemed like a nice place to move to."

Sally's eyebrows rose at the tone in Sarah's voice, as if she were in some kind of trouble, and she wondered how Sarah would have heard of Big Rock in the much larger city of Pueblo.

"I hope I'm not being too nosy, Sarah, but just why do you have to get out of Pueblo?"

When Sarah hesitated and stared past Sally out the window as the train began to move out of the station, Sally patted her on the arm. "Never mind, dear," Sally said, turning and looking forward. "Your reasons are none of my business and I fear I'm intruding on your privacy."

Sarah, not wanting to make Sally suspicious, decided to tell her the story she'd made up to account for her moving from Pueblo to Big Rock.

"Oh, don't worry, Sally, it's nothing all that mysterious," Sarah said, making her voice light and carefree. "It's just that I was engaged, until recently, to a prominent member of Pueblo society. When we decided to cancel our engagement, people began to talk, and my family thought it best if I moved away, for at least a little while, to let matters settle down," she finished.

"Ah," Sally said, nodding, "an affair of the heart often makes tongues waggle, especially tongues of the gossip mongers who like nothing better than to besmirch someone else's reputation." She clucked and shook her head. "Now, even though the people of Big Rock are very nice, Sarah, I wouldn't be too quick to tell anyone your story. It is after all a small town, and it does have its gossips just like all towns do."

"That's it exactly, Sally. Oh, I knew you'd understand," Sarah said, blushing in shame at deceiving this woman who was being so kind to her.

"Of course I understand, dear," Sally said. "I'm not so old that I cannot remember what it was like when my husband first began courting me, and how the gossip flew hot and heavy around my town at the time."

Sarah realized she needed to find out if Sally Jensen's husband was Smoke Jensen. She figured he was, but Jensen wasn't all that uncommon a name and she wanted to be sure. After all, she still couldn't believe someone as nice as Sally seemed to be would be married to a gunfighter like Smoke Jensen, a man who killed defenseless boys.

"Tell me about your husband, Sally," Sarah said, leaning back in her chair a bit so she wouldn't seem too anxious. "What's his name?"

Sally laughed. "Well, his name is Kirby, Sarah, but he goes by Smoke, or at least that's what everyone including me calls him."

"Smoke?" Sarah asked. "My, what an unusual name." It was him. She was married to a monster.

Sally's eyes became distant as she thought back to what Smoke had told her of his early days in the Wild West . . .

Sarah stared at Sally, who seemed lost in a pleasant memory for the moment. This wasn't what she'd expected. Most gunmen, at least all that she'd been acquainted with or told about, didn't have wives. They were for the most part a sorry lot of drunkards and malcontents who drifted from one place to another, selling their guns and their willingness to kill without reason to the highest bidder. And the women they did take up with, when they weren't busy killing, were nothing like Sally Jensen. Why, she and I could be friends if things were different, Sarah thought wryly. I just can't believe she's married to a man as evil as Smoke Jensen and doesn't realize how bad he really is.

After a moment, Sarah reached over and gently touched Sally's arm. "Mrs. Jensen," she said tentatively.

Sally started and seemed to come out of her reverie. "Oh, excuse me, Sarah," she said, smiling almost sadly. "I fear my long journey has tired me considerably and I was daydreaming for a moment."

"No, that's all right," Sarah said, returning the smile. "You seemed to be someplace else for a minute . . . someplace nice."

"I was just remembering some tales my husband told me of his first days out here in the wilderness, back when he was no more than a child."

"Oh?"

"Yes. Things were very different then, and Smoke had to learn to use both his wits and his guns at a very young age." Sally laughed softly. "Thank goodness we're much more civilized nowadays and things are different."

Not so different as you think, Sally, not so different at all, Sarah thought, struggling to keep the hatred she felt for Smoke from showing in her eyes or in her voice.

Five

Sarah decided it would be best if she could find out all she could about this man she planned to kill, this man who went by the unlikely name Smoke. She didn't like taking advantage of a nice woman like Sally, but it wasn't her fault the lady had married a monster and didn't seem to realize it. Perhaps if she could get her to talk about him, she would find out how best to get close to him and then take him out.

"Please, Sally," she said, "if you're not too tired, tell me some of those tales about your husband's early days out here and how he got such an unusual name as Smoke."

"Well," Sally said, hesitating, "I wouldn't want to bore you."

"Oh, you won't," Sarah promised. "My father used to tell my brother and me about how he got started years ago, back when things were very different in Colorado Territory, and his stories always fascinated us."

Sally smiled. "We're a lot alike, Sarah,"

she said. "I too have always been interested in the history of the Old West."

The only difference is my father is a respectable rancher and your husband is a cold-blooded killer and gunman, Sarah thought.

Sally settled back in her seat and closed her eyes, letting the memories of the stories Smoke had told her come to the front of her mind. . . .

Smoke was sixteen years old when his father returned to their hardscrabble farm in Missouri from fighting for the Gray in the Civil War. When young Kirby told his father that his mother, Emmett's wife, had died the previous spring, Emmett put the farm up for sale and he and Kirby moved off headed west.

They rode westward, edging north for several weeks, moving toward country controlled by the Kiowa and Pawnee Indians. When they arrived at the Santa Fe Trail, they met up with a mountain man who called himself Preacher. He was dressed entirely in buckskins, from his moccasins to his wide-brimmed hat. Young Kirby thought him the dirtiest man he'd ever seen; even his white beard was so stained with tobacco as to be almost black.

Soon after their meeting, the three men were ambushed by a group of Indians that Preacher said were Pawnees, and took refuge in a buffalo wallow just behind a low ridge.

Suddenly the meadow around them was filled with screaming, charging Indians. Emmett brought one buck down with a .44 slug through the chest, flinging the Indian backward.

The air had changed from the peacefulness of summer quiet to a screaming, gun-smoke-filled hell. Preacher looked at Kirby, who was looking at him, his mouth hanging open in shock, fear, and confusion.

"Don't look at me, boy!" he yelled. "Keep them eyes in front of you!"

Kirby jerked his gaze to the small creek and the stand of timber that lay behind it. His eyes were beginning to smart from the acrid powder smoke, and his head was aching from the pounding sound of the Henry .44 and the screaming and yelling. The Spencer rifle Kirby held at the ready was a heavy weapon, and his arms were beginning to ache with the strain.

His head suddenly came up, eyes alert. He had seen movement on the far side of the creek. Right there! Yes, someone was over there.

Kirby was thinking to himself that he really didn't want to shoot anyone when a young brave suddenly sprang from the willows by the creek and lunged into the water, a rifle in his hand.

As the young brave thrashed through the water toward him, Kirby jacked back the hammer of the Spencer, sighted in on the brave, and pulled the trigger. The .52-caliber pounded his shoulder, bruising it, for there wasn't much spare meat on Kirby. When the smoke blew away, the young Indian was facedown in the water, his blood staining the stream.

Kirby stared at what he'd done, then fought back waves of sickness that threatened to spill from his stomach.

The boy heard a wild screaming and spun around. His father was locked in hand-to-hand combat with two knife-wielding braves. Too close for the rifle, Kirby clawed out the .36-caliber Navy Colt from leather. He shot one brave through the head just as his father buried his Arkansas Toothpick to the hilt in the chest of the other.

And as abruptly as they came, the Indians were gone, dragging as many of their dead and wounded with them as they could. Two braves lay dead in front of

65

Preacher, two braves lay dead in the shallow ravine with the three men; the boy Kirby had shot lay facedown in the creek, arms outstretched, the waters a deep crimson. The body slowly floated downstream.

Preacher looked at the dead buck in the creek, then at the brave in the wallow with them . . . the one Kirby had shot. He lifted his eyes to the boy.

"Got your baptism this day, boy. Did right well, you did."

"Saved my life, son," Emmett said, dumping the bodies of the Indians out of the wallow. "Can't call you a boy no more, I reckon. You're a man now."

A thin finger of smoke lifted from the barrel of the Navy .36 Colt Kirby held in his hand. Preacher smiled and spit tobacco juice.

He looked at Kirby's ash-blond hair. "Yep," he said. "Smoke'll suit you just fine. So Smoke hit'll be."

"Sir?" Kirby finally found his voice.

"Smoke. That's what I'll call you now on. Smoke."*

Sarah's face was flushed and she was

*(*The Last Mountain Man*)

66

fanning herself with a small handkerchief as Sally finished her tale of how her husband came to be called Smoke and of his introduction to the Wild West.

The story had been very exciting, and somehow it reminded Sarah of the stories Cletus and her father had told her as she was growing up, about how they'd had to hold off Indian attacks and bandit attacks while still trying to raise crops and cattle and babies.

"My, my, Sally," Sarah said, taking a deep breath. "That was quite a story."

Sally smiled as she patted Sarah's thigh next to her on the seat. "Things were quite different in those days, Sarah. The Indians were still around and hated the intrusion of the white man, and there was no law to call upon when you got in trouble. People had to learn to take matters into their own hands, and they became very tough in the doing."

Kind of like me, Sarah thought as she turned her face to stare out of the window. Since the law is unable to do what is right, I'm taking matters into my own hands, and I'm going to kill Smoke Jensen for what he did to my brother.

After a moment spent composing herself and forcing her face into an expression of friendship, Sarah turned back around and faced Sally. "And did this country make your husband tough, Sally?" she asked, trying to keep the venom out of her voice and her expression pleasant.

Sally pursed her lips as she thought about the question. She didn't quite know how to answer it. True, Smoke was as tough a man when provoked as she'd ever met, but with her he was invariably gentle and kind, and she knew that there was no man more loyal to his friends than her husband, or more fearsome to his enemies. So, she guessed Smoke was tough when he needed to be and gentle and kind when he was allowed to be.

Unable to put all this into words without sounding like a fool, she just shrugged. "I suppose Smoke became as tough as he needed to be to survive in those days, but thankfully, those days are gone now and he has little need for that ability nowadays." She smiled at Sarah. "Nowadays, he spends his time with me on our ranch just outside of Big Rock, raising cattle and horses and being a boring old homebody."

She glanced over Sarah's shoulder and pointed. "And speaking of Big Rock, I do believe we're pulling into town right now."

Sarah followed Sally's gaze, hoping her

friends already stationed there wouldn't be foolish enough to try to meet her at the station. She'd told Sally she didn't know anyone in town, and she didn't want them to make a liar out of her. She realized if she was to have any chance to get close enough to Smoke Jensen to do him in, she was going to have to have the trust of his wife.

She sighed. "Well, here I go about to start a new life for myself," Sarah said. She looked at Sally. "I hope I'll be able to find a nice place to stay and a good job soon."

Sally didn't hesitate. "I'm sure that won't be a problem," she said. "I know that Ed and Peg Jackson, who own the town's largest general store, are always looking for someone to help out so that Peg can spend more time at home with the children, and there's a very nice boarding-house right on Main Street that caters to young, single women."

Sarah forced herself to smile brightly. "Oh, thank you, Sally. I don't know what I'd have done if we hadn't met."

Sally added, "Of course, if money is tight, you could always stay out at our ranch for a while until you've worked long enough to afford your own place."

Sarah paused, considering Sally's offer

for a moment. True, that it would give her plenty of access to Smoke Jensen, and would make it much easier when she finally decided to kill him, but she would be severely limited in being able to contact her friends in town or to keep in touch with her father about the details of what was going on. She finally decided against accepting Sally's offer, but she wanted to leave the door open for visits out to the ranch just in case.

"Oh, that is so kind of you, Sally, but my father made sure I had plenty of money when he sent me here. I have enough to tide me over until I get a few paydays behind me, but I would appreciate the chance to see your spread and visit with you if I get too lonely."

Sally patted her arm and stood up, getting her valise from the overhead rack. "Well, you know that you're always welcome, Sarah, and I'll be sure to have you out to dinner once you're settled in."

As they moved down the aisle when the train had ground to a halt, among much screeching of brakes and hissing of steam, Sally said, "I'll stop by the Jacksons' place on my way out of town and tell them that you'll be calling for a job."

Sarah nodded, her mind elsewhere as

she searched the small crowd on the platform looking for either Carl Jacoby or Dan Macklin. If she saw them, she was going to have to give them some sign to stay away until they could meet later, when no one was around to see them.

Fortunately, there were no familiar faces in the group waiting on the platform, and Sarah let herself relax as she handed a porter her claim ticket for her luggage.

Still, it wouldn't hurt to be extra careful. Sarah decided to take her time exiting from the train so she wouldn't be next to Sally in case her friends were out there waiting for her.

She went back into the ladies' parlor room, and pretended to be fussing with her hat and dress in front of the mirror, giving Sally plenty of time to leave the car ahead of her.

Six

Sally too was anxiously scanning the crowd, looking for her husband as she stood on the platform, her heart beating a little faster than usual in her anticipation of seeing and holding him again.

Just as she was about to give up, thinking that perhaps he hadn't gotten her wire stating her arrival day, she saw him on the edge of the crowd, leaning up against the wall of the station house.

Gosh, but he looks good, she thought, flushing at the sight of his wide shoulders, heavily muscled arms, and tanned, handsome face. Even though his ash-blond hair was beginning to be streaked with touches of gray at the temples, he was still the best-looking man she'd ever seen, and the most desirable to boot.

She was glad to note the way his eyes lit up and his lips curled in a wide grin when he spied her. She dropped her valise and ran into his arms, inhaling the musky man-scent of him and sighing deeply with contentment. She was where she belonged, finally, and it had been a long time since she'd felt so safe and happy. She wondered briefly if he could feel the way her heart beat wildly in her chest at the touch of his arms around her.

She leaned back and looked up at his hair. Usually unruly, with a lock or two falling down over his forehead in a most appealing manner, it was shiny and slicked back and smelled faintly of pomade.

She grinned at him. "I see you've changed your hair," she said, running her hands through it and mussing it up just as she liked it.

He blushed. "Oh, I thought I'd get a trim in honor of your arrival, so I let the barber whack a little bit off the sides." He winced. "He put that smelly stuff in it before I could stop him, and I didn't have time to wash it out 'fore your train was due to arrive."

She locked an arm in his and walked with him toward the baggage car to collect her luggage. "Well, don't worry. I'll heat us up some water when we get to the Sugarloaf and we'll have a bath."

He turned to her, a slight flush on his face. "We?" he asked.

She too blushed. "Of course. I have to wash the grime of my journey off, and you

have to get that pomade out of your hair."
She hesitated. "If we share the bath, you
won't have to work so hard to bring extra
water into the cabin," she said, her face
bright red at the brazenness of her pro-
posal. Not that they hadn't shared an inti-
mate bath before. It was just that they
didn't usually discuss it out in public beforehand.

He smiled slowly. "So, I see that you've
missed me as much as I've missed you."

She cocked one eye up at him. "More!"
was all she said, but her tone caused him
to rush the porter to get her luggage and
put it on the buckboard so they could get
back to the Sugarloaf as soon as possible.
He had some serious welcoming-home to
attend to, and he wasn't sure he could wait
the few hours the trip home would take!

Sally looked around at the crowd of
people near the baggage car, hoping to see
Sarah. She wanted to introduce Smoke to
her new friend, but Sarah was nowhere to
be seen. Oh well, Sally thought, there'd be
plenty of time for that later.

She made a mental note to tell Smoke to
be sure and stop by the general store on
their way out of town so she could tell Peg
Jackson about the girl who wanted to work
there. Peg would be ecstatic, since that

would allow her more time at home with their children.

At that very moment, standing only a couple of dozen feet behind Smoke and Sally, Sarah put her hand in her handbag and closed her fingers around the butt of a snub-nosed Smith and Wesson .36-caliber revolver. Her eyes narrowed as she saw for the first time the man who'd killed her brother. Her heart beat fast, and she began to tremble at the sight of the monster who'd ruined her family. Perhaps it would be best to get it over with and kill him now. After all, she might never get a better chance.

She started to pull the weapon out and put a bullet in the back of his head, but a hand closed over her arm.

She whirled around, her hate-filled eyes glaring as Carl Jacoby whispered in her ear, "Not here and not now, Sarah. Don't be a fool."

She struggled against his grip for a moment, and then she relaxed as the killing fever left her. She slumped against him and let him pull her out of sight around the corner of the station building.

"You're right, Carl," she said as he leaned her back against the wooden wall.

"A shot in the back with no warning would be too easy for that man. I want to look into his eyes when he knows he's about to die and tell him just why I'm going to kill him. I want him to suffer, to think about never seeing his wife again, to know what his dastardly act in Pueblo cost him."

Carl glanced around to make sure no one was watching. Sarah was really worked up, with her red face and animated talk. He knew he'd better get her out of sight before someone came up and asked what was going on.

"Come on, Sarah. I've got a room reserved for you at the hotel."

She stopped him with a hand on his chest. Nice girls didn't stay at hotels, especially by themselves without any other family around.

"Uh-uh, Carl. I think I'll get a room at a boardinghouse Mrs. Jensen recommended to me."

"What?" he asked, his eyes wide and his face paling at her words. "What do you mean Mrs. Jensen . . . ?"

Sarah smiled, calmer now that her thoughts of an immediate kill were over, and she began to walk up the street. "I'll explain it all to you later, over dinner." She looked at him. "This place does have an acceptable eating establishment, I take it?"

He nodded, his expression worried. He still couldn't believe she'd been talking to Smoke Jensen's wife on the train. He hoped she hadn't given anything away. He knew that if the people of this town thought that anyone was going to try and harm their favorite son, Smoke Jensen, they'd most likely string them up from the nearest maple tree.

Cal and Pearlie were lying around the bunkhouse, mending socks and sewing buttons on shirts and doing all the things that needed doing after a few months away from home, when they heard the buck-board pull up in front of the ranch house.

Cal jumped to his feet and looked out the window. "Hey, Pearlie," he called, turning with a big grin on his face as he headed for the door. "It's Smoke and Sally."

"Hold on, pard, just where do you think you're goin'?" Pearlie drawled from his place at the table next to the potbellied stove.

Cal stopped and looked back over his shoulder. "Didn't you hear me, Pearlie? Miss Sally's back from her trip," he said. "I'm gonna go out there an' tell her hello."

Pearlie grinned and shook his head. "No, you're not, young'un," he said firmly.

Cal put his hands on his hips. "And just why not?" he asked angrily. "It's been almost a year since I seen her and I want'a tell her how much I missed her."

"Son, I know you ain't had a whole passel of experience with womenfolk like I have, so I guess I'll just have to excuse your ignorance on the subject and maybe try an' explain a few things to you."

Cal raised his eyebrows and moved toward Pearlie. "And just what does my experiences with females have to do with anything, 'ceptin' your dirty mind?"

Pearlie sighed and took a drink from his coffee mug that was sitting on a small pine table next to his bunk, along with some spare change, a pocketknife, and his tobacco pouch and papers.

"Think about it, Cal. Smoke and Sally have been away from each other for the better part of a year now, and they're fixin' to be alone together for the first time in a lot of months." He raised his eyebrows as if that explained everything to the young man.

"So?" Cal asked, clearly not getting Pearlie's drift. "That's what I been sayin'. Miss Sally's been gone a long time an' —"

"Do I have to spell it out for you, Cal?" Pearlie said with a heavy sigh, speaking as if he were talking to someone not quite right in the head. "Who do you think Sally wants to spend time with right now, you or Smoke?"

Suddenly, it dawned on Cal what Pearlie was trying to hint at.

"But you don't think they're gonna . . . ?" he said, his eyes wide and his face flushing bright red.

Pearlie laughed. "Well, if'n I was Smoke an' I hadn't been with my wife in over six, seven months, I sure as hell would first chance I got."

"But . . . but it's daylight outside!" Cal argued, aghast at the very idea.

Pearlie sighed again and looked down into his coffee cup, his eyes crinkling at the corners as he smiled. "Boy, do you have a lot to learn, Cal, more than you can ever imagine."

A couple of hours later, after Sally had heated enough water to fill the oversized tub they kept in their spare bedroom, and after they'd both managed to get freshened up from their trip and their rather exuberant welcome home, Smoke knocked on the bunkhouse door.

Pearlie answered it, since Cal was in the middle of trying to mend a hole in one of his socks that was almost big enough to put a fist through.

Smoke leaned inside. There was no one there except Cal and Pearlie, the other hands not in from the fields yet.

"You boys interested in some real home cooking for a change?" he asked.

Pearlie shook his head, a sorrowful expression on his face. "You don't mean you're gonna make Miss Sally cook her first night back home, do you, Boss?"

Smoke shrugged. "I offered to eat leftovers from Cookie's dinner meal, but she insisted on cooking. Said it'd been a long time since she cooked for her family and she wanted to do it."

"You sure she intended for you to ask Pearlie an' me over too, Smoke?" Cal asked from his bunk.

Smoke grinned. "When Sally said she wanted to cook for her family, who the heck do you think she meant?"

Pearlie beamed at him and Cal being included in the term family by Sally, and quickly nodded. "You bet, Smoke. Give us a few minutes to clean up an' we'll be right over."

Smoke looked back over his shoulder

and sniffed loudly through his nose. "Well, don't take too long. If my nose isn't wrong, I think her fresh apple pie is just about ready."

Pearlie's eyes opened wide and he whirled around and headed for the pitcher and washbasin in the corner, already rolling his sleeves up. He hadn't had any of Sally's wonderful home cooking for a long time and he could hardly wait.

"Course you're gonna have to wait until you finish the fried chicken and mashed potatoes and green beans and fresh-baked rolls before she's gonna let you have any of the pie," Smoke added from the doorway.

"Fried chicken?" Cal asked, licking his lips over the thought.

"And mashed potatoes and fresh green beans and oven-baked bread," Pearlie finished, his eyes dreamy as if he were talking about a lovely woman who'd just asked him out.

"Outta the way, Cal," Pearlie called as he hurried toward the door, " 'less you want'a get runned over."

Seven

Carl Jacoby carried Sarah's luggage as she walked down Main Street until they came to a white clapboard building with a sign next to the front door that read ROGERS' BOARDING HOUSE.

Sarah knocked on the door, and a rotund woman wearing a white apron sprinkled with flour answered it. She was wiping her hands on a cup towel, and looked angry at being interrupted.

"Yes?" she asked, irritation in her voice.

"Hello," Sarah said. "My name is Sarah Johnson. Mrs. Sally Jensen referred me to you. She said you rent rooms to young single ladies."

The woman in the doorway broke into a big smile, all traces of irritation vanishing immediately. "Well, howdy, Sarah," she said, sticking out her hand. "My name is Melissa Rogers, but everyone calls me Mamma. Come on in."

Sarah took the hand, which seemed as big as a ham, and shook it as she entered the door.

"You can just put the luggage down here in the parlor, boy," Mamma Rogers said to Carl Jacoby, who grimaced at the term "boy" but kept his mouth shut as he unloaded the suitcase and valise.

Sarah stepped over to him and handed him a bit of change from her purse, as if she were tipping a stranger for carrying her bags for her. With her back to Mamma Rogers, she mouthed the words "I'll see you later."

After Sarah had told Mrs. Rogers the same lie about her reasons for coming to Big Rock as she'd told Sally, Mamma showed her to a room on the second floor overlooking Main Street.

"I'm sorry 'bout this room, Sarah," Mrs. Rogers said, moving over to open the drapes and let some light into the room. "It's a mite noisy on weekends when the local cowboys are in town celebrating, but it's the last one I have available, and you do catch a nice breeze through the window."

Sarah stepped to the window and peered out. In her mind she could see herself taking careful aim with a rifle down at Smoke Jensen as he passed on the street below — it wouldn't be as gratifying as looking into his eyes as she killed him, but it would do for a backup plan in case she wasn't able to get him alone long enough to do it face-to-face.

She turned back around to Mamma, smiling, all traces of her murderous thoughts gone from her innocent visage. "Oh, this room will do nicely, Mamma, and I do like the view of Main Street."

An hour later, after she'd unpacked her luggage and paid Mamma Rogers for the first two weeks, she asked about a good place to eat.

"Well, you're welcome to eat here most nights," Mamma said, "but if you need a place to have a good home-cooked meal at lunch or breakfast, you can't beat the Sunset Café over on Second Street."

"Thank you," Sarah said. "I think I'll take a walk around town and get acquainted with my new home."

After she left Mamma Rogers's place, she stepped into the hotel where Carl had told her he was staying, and left a note with the desk clerk telling him where to meet her.

Thirty minutes later, after walking around doing some sightseeing, she joined Carl Jacoby and Daniel Macklin at the Sunset Café on Second Street. It was past lunchtime and before dinnertime, and so the place was practically deserted, which was just fine with Sarah because she didn't want too many people to see her conversing with the two new men in town.

"Hello, Daniel," she said as she approached their table, glad to see another familiar face from her hometown.

Daniel dipped his head. "Howdy, Sarah. I see you made the trip all right."

Carl, who was bursting with curiosity about her earlier comments about Mrs. Jensen, butted in. "Now, what's this about you an' Smoke Jensen's wife becomin' such good friends on the train?"

"What?" Macklin said. Jacoby hadn't told him of her comments about Mrs. Jensen.

Sarah smiled secretively as she waved the waitress over and told her she would have the lunch special and a cup of hot tea to drink.

Jacoby and Macklin had already ordered beefsteaks and fried potatoes.

After the waitress put her tea and food on the table and gave her a small jar of honey to use in her tea, Sarah told the two men what had happened on the train while she ate.

"You were taking an awfully big chance,

85

talking to Mrs. Jensen like that," Jacoby said as he picked at his steak, a worried expression on his face.

Macklin fixed him with a scornful glance as he said, "Our friend Carl here seems to have come up with a sudden lack of courage where it comes to Smoke Jensen," he said, a sneer in his voice.

Sarah raised her eyebrows and gave Carl a questioning look as she sipped her tea. "Well, Carl, for your information, I didn't know whose wife she was when we struck up a conversation, and after she told me she was married to Smoke Jensen, I couldn't very well just get up and leave, now could I?" she said.

"I guess not," he admitted, still not able to look at her.

"Now, what's this Mac is saying about you being afraid of Smoke Jensen?" she asked, her voice getting hard.

Carl, flushing, argued back, "That's not true!" He fussed with his steak for another moment. "It's just that everything I see and hear about this man don't fit the picture of a backshooter or a man who'd kill someone without giving them a fair chance."

Sarah pursed her lips and slowly put her teacup down on the table. "So," she said in a low voice, her eyes boring into Carl's. "Now you're an expert on Smoke Jensen and you think what he did when he shot my brother and your friend was all right?"

Carl shook his head. "That's not what I'm tryin' to say, Sarah," he said, a pained expression on his face as he tried to make himself understood. "It's just that I don't think it went down like everybody in Pueblo seems to say it did."

Macklin gave a short, harsh laugh. "Yeah, Sarah," he said, his voice dripping with scorn. "Carl here thinks this Jensen is so quick with a handgun he could draw and put five or six slugs in Johnny an' his friends 'fore they could even get a shot off, even though they already had their guns out."

Sarah shook her head and turned her gaze back to Carl. "Is that really what you think, Carl?"

He nodded, leaning forward and putting his elbows on the table as if by getting closer to her he could make her believe what he was saying. "You got to see him draw to believe it, Sarah. The man is fast as greased lightning."

"So was Johnny, Carl. You know that," she said, her eyes beginning to tear up at all this talk about how her brother got shot and killed.

Carl shook his head, sorry he was making her sad but determined to make his point. "No, Johnny wasn't in Jensen's class, Sarah. Johnny was quick, all right, but Jensen is as fast as I've ever seen, bar none."

Now it was Sarah's face that flushed as she leaned across the table toward Carl until their faces were inches apart. "Well, it really doesn't matter, does it?" she said in a bitter tone. "Whatever happened that day in Pueblo, Smoke Jensen put lead in my brother and then he walked away like it never happened, and for that we're going to kill him!" She hesitated, and leaned back to take a sip of her tea before adding, "Unless you really have lost your nerve like Mac says you have."

Macklin threw his napkin down on the table. "Now you're talkin', Sarah. I say we go look for him and get this over with right now."

Jacoby didn't answer her accusation; he just looked at her with lovesick eyes, knowing he'd probably lost any chance for her to ever think of him in a favorable way again.

Sarah sighed and shook her head, a thoughtful expression on her face. "No, Mac. I want this done right. When I put the fatal bullet in Smoke Jensen's heart, I want to be looking in his eyes while I do it, and that is going to take some planning."

Macklin's eyes widened. "Sarah, you can't be serious. Carl's right about one thing. From what everybody around here says, Jensen is snake-quick on the draw. You wouldn't have a chance goin' up against a man like Jensen face-to-face."

She smiled and took a delicate sip of her tea. Her eyes had a mischievous twinkle in them. "Not if he didn't know I was coming after him," she said softly.

After Sarah finished her meal and left the café, warning the boys not to approach her in public but to leave a message in the mail slot at her boardinghouse when they needed to speak, Macklin shook his head.

"That little filly's gonna get in a world of trouble the way she's goin' after Jensen," he said, a sour expression on his face.

Jacoby, who had to struggle whenever he was around Sarah not to let his feelings for her show, nodded in agreement. "Yeah, an' if anything happens to her while we're supposed to be watchin' out for her, her old man will have our hides nailed to his barn door 'fore the week's out."

Macklin leaned back in his chair and

slipped the Colt from his holster. He held the gun down out of sight from the waitress and opened the loading gate, checking the cylinders to make sure the pistol was fully loaded.

Jacoby frowned. "What the hell are you doin', Mac?"

"I'm getting ready to save Sarah and do what old man MacDougal sent us here to do in the first place — kill Jensen 'fore Sarah has a chance to get herself hurt trying that damn fool plan of hers."

Jacoby laughed harshly. "You're crazy, Mac. I done told you that you won't stand a chance against Jensen. He's too damned fast for you or me to handle." He hesitated. "Heck, I don't think we'd have a snowball's chance in hell if we drew down on him at the same time."

Macklin snorted. "Hell, Carl, I didn't say I was gonna challenge him to a duel face-to-face." He smiled grimly. "There's more'n one way to skin a cat, as they say."

"You're not going to backshoot him, are you?" Jacoby asked, his lips puckered like he'd tasted something sour at the very thought. It was only the lowest type of men in the West who would deign to shoot another man in the back, and Carl Jacoby couldn't believe Macklin would stoop that low, no matter the reason.

Macklin shook his head. "No, but I'm not gonna give him much warnin' either. I'll just walk up to him when he's not expecting any trouble and hook and draw."

"But you'll be arrested and hung."

"Naw, 'cause as soon as I fire I'm gonna hightail it outta there and be on my horse ridin' outta town 'fore he hits the floor."

Jacoby thought about it as he finished his coffee. After a moment, he said, "You might just have a chance." And even if he gets caught, at least he'll save Sarah from trying to do it herself, Jacoby thought to himself, but didn't say out loud.

Macklin slid his six-gun in its holster and then he got to his feet. "Now, let's go see if we can find Jensen," he said, wanting to get it done before he had a chance to think about it and change his mind.

Eight

Smoke was finishing his second cup of coffee at the breakfast table while Sally stood behind him, kneading his shoulders.

"Well, sir," she said, a teasing note in her voice, "how does it feel to be back from the wilds of Canada working as a boring old married rancher again instead of an intrepid explorer risking life and limb to carve a railroad out of a remote wilderness?"

Smoke laughed out loud. "Intrepid?" he asked. "Now that's a new one on me." He looked over his shoulder at her and grinned. "I suppose that means incredibly handsome and desirable?"

"No, sir, it certainly does not mean that. It means fearless, very brave," Sally, the exschoolteacher, informed him, putting on a highfalutin air.

He half-turned in his chair and pulled her down on his lap. "To tell you the truth, lady," he said, a twinkle in his eyes, "if I hadn't had you to come home to, I just might have stayed up there in the Canadian mountains." He paused, and his eyes got a faraway look in them. "They reminded me of the way it was out here twenty years ago, before all the pilgrims came from back East and spoiled it all."

"So," she said, leaning her head on his shoulder, "you gave all that up for little old me?"

He bounced her up and down a couple of times, grinning and patting her hip with his hand. "Oh, I don't know about 'little' anymore."

She straightened up with a frown. "Are you insinuating I gained weight while I was visiting my parents? That my hips are suddenly too big?" she asked, frost in her voice and her eyes flat and dangerous.

Realizing his mistake, he tried to get out of it, and of course that just made it worse. "Uh, no, dear, of course not. I was just teasing . . ."

"That does it, Smoke Jensen," she said, scrambling to her feet and smoothing her dress down over her hips. "I'm going to go on a diet right away."

"Now sweetheart . . ." Smoke began, knowing from past experience that when Sally dieted, everyone dieted. It was not a pleasant experience by any means.

She turned her back to him and began

fussing with the leftover biscuits and sausage patties on the counter. "You'd better get a move on, Smoke," she said, her voice still cool and flat. "Pearlie said there were lots of supplies you needed to go get from town."

Smoke sighed. He'd really put his foot in it this time. Why were women so sensitive about their weight? he thought. Men weren't.

He got up from the table and put his guns on. As he got ready to leave, he walked over and put his arms around her from behind, holding her breasts as he leaned down to kiss the back of her neck.

"You don't need to diet, darling," he whispered, hoping she'd relent and give him a reason to put off his trip to town. "You've got the best figure in the territory."

"Or at least the biggest," she finished, her body stiff in his arms and her neck red and flushed.

He sighed and left the kitchen. Maybe she'd be in a better mood when he got back from Big Rock with the supplies. Maybe he'd get lucky and she'd forget all this nonsense about her needing to diet.

As he walked over to the bunkhouse, he chuckled. Pearlie was going to be mighty disappointed if Sally refused to make any more pies or bear sign for a while, that was for sure.

Smoke rode his big Palouse stud while Cal and Pearlie rode in the buckboard. Pearlie, after talking to the men he'd left in charge while they went on their jaunt up to Canada, found they were in dire need of several rolls of wire, some nails, and various other assorted supplies to make the repairs that always seemed to be necessary to keep a ranch in good order.

As they rode into town, Smoke said, "I got some bad news, boys."

"What's that?" Cal asked.

"Sally thinks she's getting fat, so she's going to go on a diet."

"What?" Pearlie exclaimed. He remembered the last time Miss Sally went on a diet. He'd about turned into a rabbit, they'd eaten so many salads and greens and carrots. "Please don't tell me that, Smoke," he said, a pained look on his face. "I was just getting used to having home cooking again." He rubbed his stomach. "I don't know if I can stand to go back to eating all them greens again."

"You and me both, pal," Smoke said as they pulled up in front of the general store.

When they entered, Cal saw what he thought was the most beautiful girl he'd ever seen in his life behind the counter. Her hair was long and fell down over her shoulders, and framed a face that belonged to an angel.

"Hello, sir," she said with a smile when she saw him gawking at her. "What can I get for you?"

"Uh . . . er . . ." he stuttered, not knowing what to say since he'd plumb forgotten why they were there. All he could think of was how pretty she was and why had he never seen her before.

"Hello, miss," Smoke said, moving toward the counter. "You must be Sarah Johnson."

Sarah's eyes narrowed and a slight flush appeared on her cheeks. "Do I know you, sir?" she asked, her voice hardening and her neck stiffening.

Smoke held up his hands, a flush appearing on his face at her reaction. "I didn't mean to give offense, Miss Johnson," he said quickly, looking around to see if Peg or Ed Jackson was around to rescue him. "It's just that my wife, Sally Jensen, said she met you on the train the other day, and she told me to tell you hello when we got here."

Sarah's eyes stayed hard for a moment, and then she made a conscious effort to soften her expression. "Oh, of course, you must be Mr. Jensen," she said, sticking out her hand and forcing her lips into a cordial smile.

Smoke shook it. "Yes, I am, but my friends just call me Smoke."

Sarah forced her eyes off Smoke, lest she give away the hatred she felt for him. "And who are these gentlemen with you, Mr. . . . uh . . . Smoke."

"This is Calvin Woods, and the skinny one over there is my ranch foreman, Pearlie," Smoke said, inclining his head at the two men.

Sarah nodded her head at Pearlie and smiled demurely at Cal, causing the boy to blush furiously.

"Are you here alone?" Smoke asked, looking around the shop as he loaded his arms with supplies and piled them on the counter.

"Yes," Sarah answered. "Mr. and Mrs. Jackson took the morning off to take their children on a picnic." She glanced over at Cal, who was still standing there staring at her with his mouth half open. "Mr. Jackson said he might even do a little fishing on the creek up north of town. Mrs.

Jackson will be in later."

"They must trust you very much to leave the store in your hands all alone."

She dipped her head, embarrassed by the compliment, especially as it came from a man she was all set up to hate. "Yes, sir, I guess they do."

Cal moved up next to Smoke and also dumped a load of supplies on the counter, almost stumbling over his feet since he seemingly couldn't take his eyes off Sarah.

When the boy just stood there staring, Pearlie, standing behind him with his arms also loaded down, cleared his throat loudly. "If you don't mind, podnah," he said with a hint of a laugh in his voice, "I'd like to put these down when you're finished gawkin'."

Cal whirled around, his face bright red. He leaned forward and thrust his face out. "I ain't gawking, Pearlie, an' don't you dare say I am."

"Calvin," Sarah called, "do you want me to add those things you're holding?"

Cal turned back around and put his supplies on the counter. "Uh, yes, ma'am, but everybody just calls me Cal."

Sarah smiled, forgetting for the moment her hatred of Smoke Jensen and everyone who worked for him. Cal was very cute, she thought, and he seemed so shy she just wanted to grab him and cuddle him like a little puppy.

Her soft mood was ruined when Smoke stepped up to the counter and said, "Just put it on the Sugarloaf bill, if you would, Sarah."

When she nodded, not looking at him for fear her hatred would show in her eyes, Smoke and Cal and Pearlie began to pick up the supplies and carry them out to the buckboard in front of the store.

Once the wagon was fully loaded, Smoke climbed up on his horse and inclined his head toward Louis Longmont's saloon. "Why don't we grab lunch over at Louis's?" he asked.

"You don't have to ask me twice," Pearlie said, "though we'd better save some room for Miss Sally's bear sign. She told me yesterday she was gonna cook up a batch today."

"Uh, I wouldn't count on that, Pearlie," Smoke said as he spurred his horse toward Louis's saloon.

Pearlie slapped the reins on the butts of the horses pulling the buckboard and caught up with Smoke. "Oh, that's right. You said Miss Sally was fixin' to go on one of her diets." He looked over at Smoke.

"Now what in blazes could make Miss Sally think she was getting too fat?"

"Well, to tell the truth, it's my fault."

"What do you mean?"

"This morning I was fooling around and I teased her that she wasn't as light as she used to be."

Pearlie groaned. "Oh, no! Don't tell me you was fool enough to say somethin' like that to a woman?"

Smoke nodded. "Yep."

"Damn!" Pearlie groaned. "You 'member last time Miss Sally got to feelin' fat?" Pearlie asked.

Smoke glanced at him, wondering how any of them could forget that terrible time.

"She didn't cook no biscuits nor bear sign nor pancakes for near about two months." Pearlie shook his head in sorrow. "Greens an' carrots an' vegetables was all we had to eat, an' I swear I 'bout had to threaten the hands with my six-gun to keep 'em on the job till she got over that foolishness."

"I remember," Smoke said. He forced a hopeful look on his face. "Maybe this time she won't stay on it too long."

"Yeah, an' maybe pigs'll learn to fly too," Pearlie added morosely.

Cal gave a short laugh. "I guess ol'

Pearlie'll be findin' lots of reasons to come to town. 'Member last time, Smoke? He came to town at least ever, two or three days so's he could eat at Louis's."

"It was the only way I could keep my weight up enough to keep my pants from falling down around my ankles," Pearlie said, laughing at the memory.

"Yeah, an' you spent just about all your wages on food, so when you needed a new pair of boots you had to borrow the money from me," Cal said, laughing.

As the three men entered Louis Longmont's saloon, Daniel Macklin and Carl Jacoby watched them from an alley up the street.

"Now's my chance," Macklin said, pulling out his Colt and checking the loads once again, even though he'd just done it back at the hotel that morning. He was nervous as a cat in a roomful of rocking chairs, but he was too proud to back down now that he'd told Jacoby what he had in mind.

"You're not gonna try for him in Longmont's, are you?" Jacoby asked. "He's in there with all his friends. You won't stand a chance."

"No, I'm not gonna take him in there.

I'm gonna wait until he comes out of the batwings. His eyes won't be used to the brightness an' he'll be half blind for a minute or two. That's when I'm gonna pull iron on him. Once he's down, I'll jump on my horse and hightail it toward Pueblo."

"How will you know when he's coming out?" Jacoby asked, watching the front of the saloon. "You can't just hang around the doorway an' wait. Someone'll see you and get suspicious. Hell, you might even get arrested for loitering."

"You're right," Macklin said, his brow furrowed as he thought about how to do it. Jacoby was right. He couldn't just stand at the window peeking in, or Jensen would surely see him and get suspicious.

"I know. I'll go in an' have me a beer or two at the bar. When I see Jensen getting up to leave, I'll walk out right ahead of him and when he comes through the batwings, I'll be waitin' for him out front."

He turned to Jacoby and stuck out his hand. "I know you don't much agree with me on this, but it's the only way I can think of to keep Sarah from getting herself hurt by trying to do it herself." He paused. "Besides, I owe it to Johnny and our other friends he cut down to do something about it," he added, his voice trembling just a bit.

"I know," Jacoby said, taking his hand. "And once you're gone, I'll explain it to Sarah and send old man MacDougal a wire tellin' him you're on your way."

As Macklin nodded and turned to leave, Jacoby added, "Good luck, Mac." He thought but didn't say out loud, *you're gonna need it!*

He didn't really think he'd have to wire Angus that Macklin was on his way, for he knew as sure as shooting that Macklin was going to die this day.

Jensen hadn't survived this long by letting men surprise him outside saloons.

Nine

Louis and his chef Andre were laughing at Smoke's description of how life was going to be on the Sugarloaf with Sally on a diet. "You know, fellahs, dieting seems to make women cranky, and when Mamma's not happy, nobody's happy," Smoke said, a morose expression on his face. "I just can't believe it," he added. "I come back from six months out in the wilderness eating with mountain men and trappers" — he paused and looked at them — "and you have no idea of just how bad that can be, and then I come home and say something stupid and kill any chance I have of getting something good to eat for a change."

"Well, my friend, from what you've told me," Louis observed dryly, "it's your own fault she feels like she has to lose weight."

"I know, I know," Smoke said. "Why couldn't I keep my big mouth shut?" He looked around, seeking support. "I was just teasing. Hell, Sally isn't fat. In fact, she's trim compared to most other women her age."

Louis laughed and shook his head while holding up his hand. "Now hold on, Smoke boy. Don't tread on that snake."

"What do you mean?"

"A woman is even more concerned with age than with weight, so don't ever say 'a woman of your age' to Sally."

The men at the table all laughed at this, realizing Louis was correct. "In fact," Louis added, "were you to make such a grievous mistake, I predict you'd not only not be eating, you'd not be doing anything else with Sally for quite some time, if you get my drift."

Smoke nodded. "Yeah, I know. Sleeping in the bunkhouse. Wouldn't be the first time either."

Andre interrupted the banter. "Monsieur Smoke, I will gladly make up a series of box lunches for you and the boys. You can send Cal or Pearlie into town every few days, and they can take them out to the Sugarloaf where you can sneak into the bunkhouse for a snack whenever you get to feeling weak from lack of sustenance."

Smoke was about to reply when he noticed a tall, heavyset man at the bar watching him while trying not to show it. Years of living as a fugitive from some untrue wanted posters had taught Smoke to listen to his instincts, and they were screaming at him to be careful of this man.

While the others at the table gave Andre their orders, Smoke leaned back in his chair, extended his right leg under the table, and unhooked the rawhide hammer thong on his right-hand Colt.

Whenever he glanced in the cowboy's direction, he noticed the man was sweating up a storm, though the temperature in the saloon was mild and cool.

Uh-huh, Smoke thought to himself, he's definitely up to something. Probably trying to get up the nerve to come over here and call me out. He'd seen this kind of behavior before, mainly when some young buck had bragged to his friends that he could take the famous gunfighter Smoke Jensen and then they'd had the effrontery to call him on it.

They usually sweated like a pig until they finally either got up the nerve to actually try their hand, or ran out in the alley and puked their guts out. He hoped this man was a puker instead of a caller. He had no desire to kill anyone today, especially someone he didn't even know.

While Cal and Pearlie and Louis reminisced over some of their adventures of the previous six months in Canada, Smoke kept his attention riveted on the man at the bar, but he did it so the man didn't know he'd been seen.

The other thing Smoke noticed that made him even more certain the cowhand was up to something was the fact that the man nursed one beer for almost thirty minutes, not ordering another but not leaving the bar either. In Smoke's experience, men at a bar either drank continually or they left. They didn't stand around sneaking looks while they sipped a beer until it was warm and flat.

Once the meal was served, Louis, who was almost as experienced in the ways of the gun as Smoke was, leaned over and said in a low voice, "What is going on, my friend?"

Smoke raised his eyebrows as he cut into the incredibly juicy and tender steak Andre had prepared. "What do you mean?" he asked, his voice innocent.

Louis smiled, though there wasn't a lot of mirth in it. "I've been watching the man at the bar, and he seems inordinately interested in you and what you're doing. Do you recognize him — perhaps someone you've come across before or someone who perhaps has a grudge against you for some reason or other?"

Smoke shook his head. "No, not that that means much. He could be a relative of someone I've had trouble with, or he could be a young gun looking to get a reputation the quick way. I just don't know."

Louis shook his head. "No, I don't think he's a gunny. He has the look of a working cowboy to me, not someone who's riding the owlhoot trail." Louis reached across the table to get the silver coffeepot, and used the act of refilling his coffee cup to observe the man better.

"In fact," Louis said as he took a drink of his coffee, "his gun is old and worn and his boots are dirty. This man is no gunslick out to make a name for himself. He doesn't dress well enough."

"Yeah, I know. I agree," Smoke said, "but he's sure as hell on the prod for me, for whatever reason."

Louis leaned back and pulled a long, black cigar from his coat pocket. As he put a match to it, he looked over the glowing tip at Smoke. "Well, what are you going to do about this impasse we find ourselves in, partner? You're not going to let him pick the time and place, are you?"

Smoke smiled at Louis. "No, you're right, Louis. That wouldn't be very smart."

Since he didn't know if the man had

friends waiting outside, Smoke looked around the table until he had Cal and Pearlie's attention. "Boys," he said in a low voice while keeping his expression bland and innocent, "keep your gun hands empty and keep a watch on the door for me. There's a gent over at the bar that's been eyeing me and I'm going over to have a talk with him. Watch my back in case he's got friends outside."

Cal and Pearlie nodded. "You got it, Boss," Pearlie said, letting his hand drift down to release his hammer thong while he continued to stuff his face using his left hand.

Smoke took a final sip of coffee and got up from the table. Before the man at the bar could move, Smoke turned and walked directly toward him.

As he approached, Smoke noticed sweat dripping from under the man's hat and running down the sides of his face. When he dropped his gaze to the man's right hand, he saw it had a fine tremor in it. The man was definitely on edge, and Smoke knew such men, though rarely effective, were still extremely dangerous because one never knew what they were going to do.

Smoke walked up and stood at the bar next to the man, facing forward with his elbows on the bar and his chin in his hand while he watched him in the mirror behind the bar.

"What do you want?" the man asked, his voice hoarse and gruff, his legs fidgety as he shifted his weight from one foot to the other and wiped sweat off his brow.

"Well, now, that's exactly the question I was fixing to ask you, friend," Smoke said, keeping his voice friendly while turning slightly so he was facing the man.

"Why . . . uh . . . what do you mean by that?"

Smoke smiled gently, his eyes interested but showing no animosity or anger. "You've been watching me for the past half hour, and you're sweating like a racehorse, so I thought I'd just end the suspense and come over here and introduce myself. I'm Smoke Jensen."

The man scowled. "I know who you are, Jensen," he growled as he picked up his warm beer and drained the mug.

"Do you have some business with me?" Smoke asked in a level voice, with no trace of challenge or fear.

"I don't do business with killers and murderers," the man said.

Smoke shrugged. "Well, I have to admit, I've killed some men in my day, though

I've never murdered anyone, and those I've killed have all tried to kill me first."

"That's a lie!"

Smoke's face flushed. He didn't ordinarily let someone talk to him like this, but he wanted to find out what the man's beef was.

"Now ordinarily, friend, a man who spoke to me in that tone and with those words would either be flat on his back with a busted jaw, or he'd be bleeding all over the floor," Smoke said evenly, trying to control his temper. "However, you've obviously got something weighing heavily on your mind that concerns me, so I'll hold off on taking any offense for now. You want to tell me what you got stuck in your craw, Mister . . . uh . . . I didn't get your name?"

The man reached into his vest pocket and pulled out a couple of coins and threw them on the bar. "Not yet, Jensen, but when I'm ready, you'll know. And the name's Macklin, Daniel Macklin."

Smoke sighed and stepped away from the bar. "Well, we can settle this right now, if that's what you really want," he said, his eyes flat and hard. His hands hung loose by his thighs, his expression expectant.

Macklin's eyes strayed to the table across the room, where Cal and Pearlie and Louis

111

all sat watching the show.

"Yeah, with your friends over there all set to gun me down if I make a play. No, thanks."

"My friends won't interfere if it's a fair fight," Smoke said, his eyes never leaving Macklin's.

Macklin sneered. "That's not the way I hear it, Jensen. In fact, I hear they usually take a hand and join right in when you kill someone."

Smoke frowned. He had no idea what this Macklin was talking about. "Mister, I don't know what you're getting at or where you get your information, but I'm telling you flat out that's a lie, and I'm willing to back my words up any way you choose." Smoke waited just a beat. "Are you?"

Macklin let his hand drop to his side, and before he could blink, Smoke's Colt was in his hand, cocked, and pointing at his chest from a distance of two inches.

Macklin's face turned pale and he took a step back. He'd never seen anything like it. He hadn't even seen Jensen's hand move before it was holding a gun.

Macklin slowly raised his hands. "You gonna shoot me down in cold blood too, Jensen?" he managed to croak through a throat that was suddenly very dry.

Smoke shook his head and holstered his gun. "I still don't know what you're talking about."

Macklin turned and walked away, saying over his shoulder, "Well, I'll be sure and remind you next time we meet."

Smoke watched him leave the saloon, and then he went back to the table and took his seat.

"You find out what he wanted?" Louis asked.

Smoke shook his head. "No, but he's got a powerful hate for me going on. Seems to think me and my friends shot someone close to him down in cold blood."

"Where'd he get that crazy idea?" Cal asked.

Smoke shrugged. "He wouldn't say."

"You don't think it's about that fracas we had up in Canada, do you?" Louis asked.

Smoke shook his head. "No, I don't see how anyone could think we were the aggressors in that fight."

"Well, like you say, he's got a powerful hate on," Pearlie said, glancing at the batwings. "I could see it in his eyes."

"Yeah," Cal added, a worried look on his face as he stared at the batwings the man had just pushed through. "I'd sure watch my back if I was you, Smoke. A man as pissed off as that man is ain't gonna think twice 'bout shooting you in the back."

Ten

Carl Jacoby, who was watching the doorway to Longmont's Saloon from an alley down the street, was astonished when Dan Macklin walked hurriedly out of the bat-wings, jumped on his horse, and hightailed it around the far corner onto a back street leading to their hotel. His back was stiff and he didn't even glance behind him as he rode away like his pants were on fire.

Carl had been expecting some fireworks from Macklin, but he hadn't heard any gunshots and there didn't seem to be a crowd forming or anyone coming out of the door looking for Macklin. Couldn't have been much of a gunfight with this little a reaction.

"Well, I'll be damned," he muttered to himself as he turned and walked quickly up the alley toward the hotel's back entrance, hoping to find Macklin and find out what had gone on in the saloon. He could tell something had happened from the way Macklin looked as he rode down the street, but he couldn't imagine what it could be.

When he got to the rear of the hotel, he saw Macklin's horse tied to a hitching rail there and the back door partially open.

He went inside, and stopped as he passed the doorway to the hotel bar when he saw Macklin standing at the bar with a bottle of whiskey in front of him and a glass to his lips.

Jacoby moved next to him at the bar, noticing his face was flushed and he was covered with sweat. His hand holding the glass was shaking so much that Jacoby was afraid Macklin would spill it all over himself if he tried to drink from it.

Without speaking, Jacoby took the whiskey bottle, poured himself a small drink, and stood there as he sipped, waiting for Macklin to speak and wondering just what the hell had happened to shake his friend up so.

After a moment, and after he'd slugged down another drink, without spilling too much, Macklin turned toward Jacoby and leaned his elbow on the bar. "Carl, you were right 'bout Jensen." He shook his head. "I ain't seen nothin' like it in all my born days."

"What happened in there, Mac?" Jacoby asked, wondering how Macklin had been able to see Jensen's draw since he hadn't heard any gunfire.

Macklin poured himself another drink, but this time he sipped it instead of swallowing it down in one gulp. "I think the man must have eyes in the back of his head. I followed him and his friends into the saloon, and I took up a station at the bar and commenced to drink me a beer while I kept a look on him out of the corner of my eye. He must've noticed me watchin' him or something, 'cause he come over to the bar where I was standin' and he braced me."

"What do you mean?"

"He asked me what was it I wanted. When I didn't exactly answer his question and I accidentally let my right hand move toward my gun, he drew his pistol."

Jacoby let his lips curl in a small smile, knowing what was coming next. "Pretty fast, huh?"

"Fast ain't exactly the word I'd use, Carl. More like lightning, I think. One second I was looking in his eyes, as cold and black as a snake's, an' the next second his hand was full of iron and I was staring down the barrel of a Colt — and the thing is, I didn't even see his hand move." He took another sip of whiskey, his hand more stable now.

"You know how when you're facing

somebody an' they're fixin' to draw, you can usually see a twitch of their arm muscle or a shift in their eyes 'fore they hook and draw?" he asked, his face pale.

Jacoby nodded. He knew what Mac meant. There was almost always some telltale sign before a man committed himself in a gunfight. Knowing this and recognizing it was what gave professional gunfighters the edge in such contests.

"Well," Macklin continued, "there was nothing about Jensen that even hinted he was going for his gun. One minute he's looking me in the eye, just talking as natural as you please, and the next he's somehow got a gun in his hand stuck against my chest and his eyes are hard and black as flint."

Jacoby's eyes narrowed. "And he didn't threaten you or hit you or anything like that after he drew his pistol and had the drop on you?"

Macklin shrugged, dropping his gaze to stare into his whiskey. "Who needs to threaten when you can draw a six-killer like that?"

"But Mac," Jacoby said earnestly, "can't you see what I've been trying to tell you? Jensen ain't no cold-blooded killer. He had the drop on you in front of his friends. If he was a showboat or looking to impress 'em, he could've pistol-whipped you or even shot you down. Hell, this is his town. No one would've blamed him. But he didn't."

Macklin's expression became thoughtful. "No, he didn't, an' you're right. There wasn't nothin' I could do to stop him from doing whatever he wanted to."

Jacoby turned back to the bar and downed the rest of the whiskey in his glass. "Maybe we'd better try and talk some sense into Sarah, or at least get her to hold off until we can figure out what we got to do."

Macklin smirked and drained his glass in one long swallow. "Hell, there ain't no need in worryin' ourselves over that, Carl, my friend. Old Man MacDougal wants Jensen dead, an' so does his daughter Sarah. As far as them two are concerned, once they've made up their minds on something, it's as good as gold."

"But maybe we can convince them they're wrong about him," Jacoby argued.

Macklin laughed. "You ever try to tell Sarah anything she didn't want to hear, boy?"

Jacoby nodded. "Yeah, I see what you mean. She is a mite stubborn at times."

"No, Carl. A mule is a 'mite' stubborn. Sarah is full-on-all-the-time stubborn."

"So, what are we gonna do?"

Macklin sighed. "I guess we got to do like you say and at least try to make her see reason." He chuckled. "Hell, worst she can do is chew our ears off."

"Maybe if we get her to hold off for a while and to watch how Jensen operates around town. Maybe she'll start to see that he ain't exactly the monster she thinks he is."

"I still think we're whistlin' in our hats, but like you say, it won't hurt to try and talk some reason into her, though the words reason and woman don't ordinarily belong together."

Macklin headed on over to the café while Carl walked to the general store down the street. Once inside, he caught Sarah's eye, mouthed the words "Sunset Café," and then left, hoping she'd understand that he needed to talk to her.

Sarah waited until Carl had been gone for a few minutes and then she went over to Peg Jackson, who was stocking a shelf in the rear of the store.

"Peg," she said, "I'm going to go over to the Sunset Café and get some coffee. I'm a little sleepy today and I need something to pick me up. Would you like for me to bring you back a cup?"

"That would be delightful, Sarah, and could you also get me a piece of one of those sweet cakes they make so well over there?"

"Certainly," Sarah said, and she took off her apron and walked down the block and around the corner to the café.

Carl and Dan were sitting in a corner booth toward the back away from any windows. Macklin didn't want to be seen with Sarah now that he'd managed to arouse Jensen's suspicions.

Sarah joined them at the table after making sure that no one she knew was in the place. After the waitress had taken their orders and placed coffee for all of them on the table, Sarah spoke. "Now, what's so all-fired important that you wanted to meet here in the middle of the day where everyone in town can see us together?"

Jacoby sat back, waiting for Macklin to speak. "Well, I had a talk with Jensen today," Macklin said.

"You what?" she exclaimed, almost yelling. When several patrons turned to glance at her, she sat back and tried to

121

calm herself down. "What did you do, Mac?" she asked in a calmer tone of voice, but it was clear she was still furious.

"Don't get upset, Sarah," Macklin said, shushing her as he looked around to make sure no one was watching them any longer. "I didn't tell him anything. I just wanted to get a feeling for the feller, that's all."

Sarah's face was flushed with anger. "And did you, Mac?" she asked in a lower voice this time. "Did you get a feeling for the man who killed my brother?"

Macklin glanced at Jacoby, who nodded, and then he leaned forward, speaking earnestly. "Yes, I think I did, Sarah, an' I don't think he did what everybody in Pueblo thinks he did."

She sat back, a look of astonishment on her face. "You don't think he shot Johnny down?"

Macklin also sat back, trying to think how he could convince her of what he felt was the truth. "Oh, I think he probably shot Johnny," he said. "But I don't think it was in cold blood or that he ambushed him. Jensen is too fast to have to do that. In fact, he's plenty fast enough to have killed Johnny and all the others in a fair fight."

Her mouth fell open in astonishment.

"And just how did you determine this, Mac?" she asked sarcastically. "Did you walk up to him and say, 'By the way, Mr. Jensen, I'd sure like to see how fast you are on the draw. Could you oblige me and show me your moves?' "

Macklin flushed in embarrassment. He wasn't used to anyone talking to him like this, especially not young women who were still wet behind the ears. "No, Sarah, I didn't do that. I just prodded him a little until he drew on me. That's when I saw how fast he was, and believe me, it was plenty fast."

Sarah looked around, shaking her head. "I don't believe this," she muttered, as if to herself. Then she looked up and stared into Macklin's eyes. "Let me remind you of something you've evidently forgotten, Mac. You work for my dad, and he sent you here for one reason, and that is to kill Smoke Jensen or to guard my back while I do it. Isn't that right?"

Macklin nodded reluctantly. "Yes, but I think Angus and you are both wrong about what happened that day. And if Jensen killed Johnny in a fair fight, which Johnny probably started, then I don't think Jensen should be killed for it."

Sarah slowly sipped her coffee, her eyes

burning into Macklin's. After a moment, she turned her gaze to Jacoby.

"Is this how you feel also, Carl?"

Jacoby nodded. "Yes, it is, Sarah. We've both looked into this before you got here, and everyone in this town thinks Jensen is straight as an arrow. They don't have one bad thing to say about him, and no one in this town would ever believe he's a backshooter or ambusher."

"Well, I'll tell you what I think," she said, her voice low and hard. "I think you're both full of . . . well, hot air."

Jacoby reached his hand across the table and tried to put it on hers. "We just don't want you going off half-cocked, Sarah, and either killing an innocent man or getting yourself shot up."

Sarah moved her hand away from Jacoby's, her lips tight. "This is going to take some thinking about," she said. "I'll send a wire to my dad and see what he thinks about all this. I may have to ask him to send me some more help, men who know their place and are loyal to him."

"Be careful what you say in a telegram," Macklin warned. "Remember, everyone in this town knows Smoke Jensen."

"Don't you worry about that, Mac. You got other things to be worried about, like what my daddy's going to say when I tell him you've gone over to the other side."

"Aw, Sarah," he said, but she held up her hand.

"Now, get out of here, the both of you. I've got some thinking to do."

After they left, she called the waitress over and ordered two pieces of the sweet cakes. One for Peg and one for her.

While she waited for her order, she sat there thinking on how she could word a telegram so her daddy would know what was going on without letting the telegrapher know what she was doing.

As she sat there, she wondered just what it was about Smoke Jensen that enabled him to fool so many people into thinking he was a good man. It never crossed her mind that perhaps they were right about him and that she and her father were wrong.

Eleven

Cletus Jones pulled his mount to a stop in a cloud of dust in front of the MacDougal ranch house and jumped to the ground. He had a feeling the telegram he'd picked up in Pueblo from Sarah MacDougal was important enough to need Angus's immediate attention.

Cletus had been MacDougal's foreman for as long as he could remember. They'd both come out here to Colorado Territory back when there were more Indians than white men, and had fought hard to carve a ranch out of the wilderness.

Cletus had been best man for Angus MacDougal's wedding, and he was godfather to both of the old man's children — now there was only Sarah since Johnny was dead.

As he ran through the front door, Mrs. MacDougal called out, "Cletus, don't you go running on my hardwood floors that've just been waxed!"

He tipped his hat and smiled, but didn't slow down appreciably as he headed toward the study/office where Angus could always be found this time of day.

Angus swiveled around in his leather high-backed chair and regarded Cletus with raised eyebrows. "Who lit a fire under your saddle, boy?" he asked in his rough, gravelly voice. Cletus was just about the only man on the ranch that Angus would allow to burst in on him unannounced.

"I got this here message from Miss Sarah, Boss," Cletus said, pulling a wrinkled yellow envelope from his breast pocket. It was wet with sweat from his rapid ride from town. "The telegraph man said it came in yesterday but it was too late to get it out here by then."

Angus frowned, but didn't say anything as he slit the envelope with a thumbnail and pulled out the telegram. At first, he'd been very angry at her for taking off after Smoke Jensen on her own without consulting him. But after thinking about it, he'd realized he would have expected a son to do it, and Sarah had always been as good as, and often better than, his son had been at managing the ranch.

He smiled and opened up the folded yellow sheet of paper. After a moment spent reading it, he swiveled around and stared out the window, thinking.

Cletus was bursting with curiosity to find out what Sarah had done about Smoke Jensen, but he knew better than to interrupt the old man while he was thinking. Even though Cletus had been with Angus MacDougal since the early days when they'd fought off Indians and rustlers and road agents together while founding the MacDougal spread, and even though he was the kids' godfather, since they were pups he'd never thought much of Johnny. He knew he was and always had been a spoiled brat. However, Cletus thought Sarah was one of the prettiest and nicest womenfolk he'd ever known. Hell, if he'd been twenty years younger and hadn't been like family to her, he'd've made a run at her himself.

After a moment, Angus turned his chair back around, crumpling the paper in his fist. "Get your gear together and gather up the best ten men you can find, Cletus. You're gonna take a little trip down to Big Rock."

When Cletus nodded, Angus turned back to his desk and picked up a pencil and paper. "And send little Jimmy in here. He's gonna need to ride to Pueblo and send my daughter an answer to her wire."

"Uh, Boss, what do I tell the men we're

gonna go to Big Rock for?" Cletus asked.

Angus MacDougal smiled grimly. "Tell 'em you're gonna go down there and pick up a skunk and bring him back here to me to deal with."

"Yes, sir," Cletus said, though he really didn't understand just what the old man meant about picking up a skunk. Hell, they had plenty of those around here if'n he wanted one.

Cletus was loyal to the bone, but sometimes he was dumb as a post.

Three days later, days Macklin spent holed up in his hotel room lest he run into Smoke Jensen or one of his friends again, a bellboy knocked on the door to Jacoby's room and handed him a handwritten note.

Jacoby opened it and read: "Meet me at our usual dining place after the noon rush at three o'clock." It was signed with only an S.

Jacoby tipped the boy a nickel and went next door and knocked on Macklin's door. When he answered, Jacoby showed him the note. "We've got about an hour till three o'clock. That ought to give you time to get freshened up a mite," Jacoby said, wrinkling his nose as he looked at Macklin's disheveled attire and unshaven face.

His friend had been in a funk ever since the day Jensen scared him half to death by drawing on him and Sarah had chewed his butt about going against her father's wishes.

"Yeah, all right," Macklin said in a dull voice.

"You got to snap out of it, man," Jacoby said. "We got work to do." He knew that Macklin was still ashamed that he hadn't had the courage to draw down on Jensen when he had the chance. Jacoby had tried to explain to him that it wouldn't have done any good, and that the only result would have been that Mac would now be deader than yesterday's news. Still, his friend was not accustomed to backing down from anyone, least of all the man who'd killed his best friend and his boss's son.

"That is, if I ain't been fired," Macklin said, and shut the door in Jacoby's face.

It was five after three and the Sunset Café was almost deserted when Macklin and Jacoby joined Sarah at their usual table in the rear. Jacoby was thankful that Macklin had shaved and washed up before the meeting. He didn't want Sarah to see how his friend had declined in mental attitude since his run-in with Smoke Jensen.

Sarah had already ordered, so the men sat down across the table from her and told the waitress to just bring them whatever she was having, though they both wanted coffee instead of the hot tea she favored.

After the waitress left, Sarah placed a telegram on the table so they could both read it. It said:

I AGREE FULLY WITH YOUR IDEA STOP WILL SEND SOME MEN TO HELP YOU ROUND UP STOCK AND BRING THEM BACK HERE TO RANCH FOR FURTHER EXAMINATION AND FINAL DETERMINATION OF THEIR DISPOSITION END

Macklin raised his eyebrows. "Just what does this mean, Sarah?"

She took a bite of her food and washed it down with her hot tea. "I telegrammed my father and told him I was having trouble rounding up the stock he was interested in and that I needed some more help, and that the beeves should be transported to the ranch rather than being slaughtered here." She inclined her head at the paper on the table. "You can see his reply for yourselves."

Jacoby leaned forward. "So what are you saying? Your dad's gonna send some men here to take Jensen prisoner and bring him back to the ranch in Pueblo?"

She smiled and wiped her mouth with a napkin. "Yes, that's exactly what it means. I didn't figure the three of us would be able to get the drop on Jensen and get him all the way back to Pueblo by ourselves." She hesitated, glaring at them through narrowed eyes. "Especially considering the rather friendly feelings toward him you two have been showing."

"Sarah," Macklin said, shaking his head. "This is crazy. Kidnapping is a hanging offense."

"So is murder, in case you've forgotten what he did to my brother," she snapped in reply. After a moment, she took a deep breath and tried to calm herself. She needed their help, and there was no need getting them so angry they might refuse it.

"Besides, since both of you seem to have some notion that Jensen is not guilty where it comes to my brother's death, I would think that you'd be glad Daddy has consented to us bringing Jensen out to the ranch and letting him tell his side of it."

Jacoby and Macklin glanced at each other. They both knew that wasn't the reason old Angus MacDougal wanted Jensen brought to him — it was more likely so the old man could have the pleasure of putting a bullet in Jensen himself, or worse, torturing the poor son of a bitch. Knowing the old man as they did, they didn't figure he'd just shoot Jensen and be done with it without first causing the man a good deal of pain and humiliation. Angus had been around long enough to have fought Indians in the old days, and to hear him tell it, he'd learned some interesting ways to torture a man from them.

"All right, let's say for the sake of argument that you are right," Jacoby said. "Just how do you think a gang of men are going to show up here in Big Rock and not bring a lot of attention to themselves so that when Jensen disappears they are not suspected?" He shook his head. "Hell, they'd have a posse on our tails 'fore we got fifty miles."

"That's easy," Sarah said, a note of triumph in her voice as she bent her head and began to eat her meal. "They're not coming into town."

"What?"

"That's right, because you and Mac are gonna ride out on the trail from Pueblo and camp out until the men get here.

You'll tell them to wait out there until I can bring Jensen to them."

"And just how in blazes do you expect to do that little trick?" Jacoby asked, while Macklin just stared at her through bloodshot eyes.

Sarah leaned back and smiled seductively while fluffing the lace ruffles on the front of her blouse. "Well, a woman's got her ways to get a man to do what she wants."

Jacoby laughed. "Bullshit, Sarah!" he exclaimed, flushing at his use of profanity in front of a woman. "Jensen may be a lot of things, killer included, but I can tell you this, the man is no womanizer. He don't even look at other women, ever!"

Sarah blushed and went back to her meal. "Well, don't you worry, Mr. Smartaleck. You just go out there and wait for the hands my daddy is sending. I'll get Jensen there one way or another, and I'll do it so it'll be a while before anyone knows he's missing."

Jacoby and Macklin looked at each other, both thinking that Sarah had gone round the bend. There was simply no way she could get the drop on a man like Smoke Jensen, no way at all, they thought.

As they walked back to their hotel, Macklin shook his head. "Now I know I should have killed Jensen." He turned tortured eyes on Jacoby. "Sarah is gonna mess around and get herself hurt or put in jail."

Jacoby smiled grimly. "I think you underestimate Sarah, Mac. Remember, she's Angus MacDougal's daughter, an' she's always been twice as smart and four times as tough as her brother ever was."

"Yeah, but Jensen's an experienced gunslick, Carl, an' he didn't get to be as old as he is by letting anyone, girls included, get the drop on him." He sighed. "Hell, I couldn't even watch him in a crowded saloon without him knowing exactly what I was doing. The man has eyes in the back of his head and the instincts of a mountain cougar."

Jacoby shrugged. "You may be right, but I don't know what the hell we can do about it." He smiled again. "Of course, you're more than welcome to go over there an' tell Sarah she's full of beans and that you think she ought to stick to cookin' an' such an' leave the rough stuff to us real men if you want to."

This last made even Macklin throw back his head and laugh. "No, thank you, Carl, 'cause I do relish my *cojones,* and Sarah would sure as hell rip them off if I ever suggested there was something Angus MacDougal's daughter couldn't do as well as any man working for 'em."

As they walked up the stairs to their hotel room to get packed and do as Sarah had told them to, Jacoby glanced sideways at Macklin. "Tell you what, pardner. I'll bet ten dollars Sarah does get Jensen out there, an' I'll give you two-to-one odds."

Macklin shook his head. "Nope. I learned a long time ago not to waste my money bettin' against a MacDougal, male or female." He sighed as he came to his door, and looked back over his shoulder at Jacoby. "You got any idea how she's gonna do it since, like you say, Jensen don't chase no skirts?"

Jacoby gave a short laugh. "No, but knowing Sarah, I wouldn't put it past her to just walk up to him and pull a gun out of her purse and stick it in his face."

"You really think so?"

Jacoby wagged his head. "Hell, Mac, I don't know. Predictin' what a woman's gonna do is like predictin' which way a frog's gonna jump — you're gonna be wrong at least half the time."

Twelve

After Angus straightened him out on the real reason he was sending him to Big Rock, Cletus picked ten of the toughest, meanest men they had working for them on the ranch. More than a few of them had once ridden the owlhoot trail and knew their ways around firearms. A couple had even spent time in the territorial prison for murder and mayhem.

As the gang of men sat on their horses in front of his house, Angus addressed them from the front porch. "Each of you men will receive a healthy bonus for this work. In fact, I'll pay you two months' wages for what should only be a couple of weeks of easy work."

Jason Biggs, one of the men who'd done time in prison and had no compunctions about killing, called out, "What if this man Jensen should give us some trouble or try to escape?" He grinned, revealing brown cigarette-stained teeth. "You want us to shoot him if'n that happens?"

Angus stared at Biggs through flat, hard

eyes, noting that unlike most cowhands, Biggs wore his six-shooter down low on his hip. Angus shook his head. Back in the old days, punks like this would've been run out of town on a rail by the citizens. "Should any of you take it upon himself to kill this man and deprive me of the pleasure of getting my hands on him, I will personally see that you experience what one of our bulls does when it is gelded. Do I make myself clear, Mr. Biggs?"

"But what if —"

"No buts, Biggs," Angus interrupted. "There are eleven of you and you're meeting up with three more, including my daughter, Sarah. That should be more than enough to keep Mr. Jensen under control." He shook his head. "And if it's not, then God help you when I get through with you."

Biggs clamped his jaws shut and busied himself with building a cigarette.

Later, on the trail, Biggs rode up next to Cletus, who was leading the group of men.

"Clete," Biggs said.

"Yeah?"

"Did the boss tell you anything about this Jensen feller 'fore he told you to go down to Big Rock and pick him up?"

Cletus shook his head, not looking at Biggs directly. He didn't like the man and never had. If it weren't so hard to find hands to stay at work through the brutal winters of Pueblo, then he'd never have been hired. "No, Jason, he didn't." Now he turned and glanced at the man riding next to him. "Why? Do you know something?"

Biggs nodded. "Yeah, I heard of this Smoke Jensen when I was in the territorial prison a while back."

Cletus continued to stare at Biggs, wondering just what the man had on his mind. Cletus didn't trust Biggs and never had, but surprisingly, he'd been a steady worker, even if he did tend to get into fights with the other hands. Luckily for him, he'd never gone so far as to pull his weapon, or he would've found out just how hard a boss Cletus could be.

"What'd you hear, Jason?" Cletus asked. He was curious about the man who'd shot Johnny. He'd heard the usual, that Jensen was pretty famous with a gun and that he'd once had some posters out on him, but that was about all he knew. He didn't get to town to listen to local gossip too often, being much too busy trying to keep the ranch going.

Biggs let his reins drop while he used both

hands to build himself a cigarette. Once he'd gotten it going, he screwed it in the corner of his mouth and let it dangle there while he talked. "Well, first off, I heard he's rattlesnake-quick with a short gun."

Cletus shrugged. "That don't surprise me none, since he somehow managed to shoot down Johnny and some of his friends, an' Johnny was no slouch with a handgun either." Smelling the smoke coming from Biggs made him want a cigarette too, so he commenced to make himself one. "Besides, there's plenty of men who're quick with a gun out here, Jason. This territory just seems to be a magnet for men who think they can make a living off their six-shooters."

Jason smirked, realizing this was directed against him, since he'd been one of those men until he'd gotten caught and sent to prison. He continued. "I also heard he's mean as a two-peckered Billy goat if you cross him or any of his friends." He inhaled and let smoke drift from his nostrils. "I shared a cell with a man who'd tried to brace Jensen once in a saloon."

Cletus laughed sourly. "If this Jensen is so fast and so mean as you say, how come the man braced him and lived to tell about it?"

Biggs smiled back. "'Cause Jensen didn't need to kill him. When my mate went for his gun, Jensen used his fists instead. He beat this guy so bad, he's gonna be eating through a straw for the rest of his life. He not only knocked all of his teeth out, he broke his jaw so bad his gums don't even come together right." Biggs laughed. "Poor sumbitch is skinny as a rail, and he used to weigh over two hundred pounds, an' he has this kind'a funny whistle when he tries to talk."

Cletus eyed Biggs. He'd never before seen Biggs give anyone the least amount of respect. "You sound like you're halfway a'feared of this man, Jason."

Biggs's face flushed scarlet and he sat up straighter in his saddle, trying to look tough. "I ain't a'scared of no man, Clete!"

Cletus wasn't fooled. He could see it in the man's eyes, lurking deep in them, like a sore that won't heal. "Well, then, why're you tellin' me all this? We're being well paid to take this little trip."

Biggs cleared his throat. "A couple of months' pay ain't so much when you're dealin' with a man like Jensen," he said, rubbing his chin with his hand.

"Well, like the boss says, fourteen of us ought'a be able to handle one man, Jason,"

Cletus said, trying to keep the scorn out of his voice. "But if you're so worried, then maybe you ought'a turn your mount around and head on back to the ranch where it's safe."

Biggs snorted through his nose. "Thirteen men, Clete, and the boss's little bitch, who looks plenty good to play in the hayloft with, but who ain't near as tough as the old man seems to think."

Before Biggs could blink, Cletus backhanded him with a fist the size of a ham, knocking him backward off his horse to land sprawling in the dirt.

When Biggs jumped to his feet and grabbed for his gun, he found himself looking down the barrel of Cletus's big Walker Colt. Cletus wasn't known as a fast draw, but he'd been handling men like Biggs for more years than he cared to think about, and he knew most of them were cowards when they didn't have an edge.

"You shouldn't ought'a talk about Miss Sarah like that, Biggs," Cletus said, his voice soft but all traces of friendliness gone from his manner. "I don't much like it, an' I hate to think of what the boss would do if'n he happened to hear about it."

Biggs relaxed and let his hand move away from his pistol. He tried a grin, but there was little humor in it and his eyes blazed with hate and humiliation. He wiped the blood off his lip with the back of his hand. "Aw, I was just funnin' with you, Clete. I know you got a soft spot for the girl. I didn't mean nothin' by what I said."

"It ain't that way, Biggs. I knowed her since she was born, so watch you mouth when you're around me, you hear?"

"Yes, sir," Biggs said, throwing an insolent half salute.

"I mean it, Jason," Cletus added, "or your friend from jail won't be the only one eating his meals through a straw."

"Is it all right if I get back on my hoss?" Biggs asked, his face flaming scarlet.

Cletus holstered his gun and leaned over in the saddle until his face was close to Biggs's. "Sure. Just don't go getting any ideas about putting a lead pill in my back, Biggs, 'cause I'm gonna tell the other men if that happens to string you up to the nearest tree. You get my drift?"

"Come on, Clete," Biggs said with a sickly smile as he climbed into the saddle. "You know we've always been friends, even if I do let my mouth override my ass ever' once in a while."

Cletus smiled back, his face equally devoid of humor. "No harm then, long as you keep your thoughts about Miss Sarah to yourself."

He jerked his horse's head around and proceeded on up the trail, whistling softly to himself while the other members of the group looked from him to Biggs, unsure of how to take this altercation.

Behind him, Biggs rode along, keeping his face bland, but his teeth were so tightly clenched together it made his jaws creak. If Cletus could have read his mind, he would not have been so cavalier about turning his back on the ex-prisoner and murderer.

Just outside the city limits of Big Rock, on the trail to Pueblo and points north, Carl Jacoby and Daniel Macklin were having some trouble. The late fall temperatures had begun to drop, and there was even the smell of snow in the air, though it was early in the year for that.

They'd stopped at the general store and bought provisions for their camp, while Sarah pretended not to know them as she waited on them with Peg Jackson working nearby. Along with foodstuffs, they'd bought a couple of small one-man tents that would keep the worst of the weather off them, though the thin oilcloth of the tents' walls would do little to keep them warm in the dropping temperatures.

Working as ranch hands and cowboys for many years, they were both experienced in camping out under the stars, but neither particularly enjoyed it, having become accustomed to the niceties of bunkhouse living over the past few years working for Angus MacDougal.

They'd also become quite accustomed to having a camp cook make their meals for them, so neither was particularly looking forward to doing their own cooking.

Jacoby gathered some hat-sized stones and made a small circle in the middle of their camp, which they'd placed on a hill overlooking the trail a quarter of a mile below them. There were some maple and oak trees in a small copse nearby that would help keep the worst of the wind off them, but it was clear that it was going to be a cold night nevertheless.

Macklin dumped an armful of deadwood he'd picked up under the trees into the campfire area, and squatted next to the stones as Jacoby put a match to some moss and dry leaves to get it going. He reached into his pocket and took out his makin's, and proceeded to build himself a cigarette as he waited for the coffeepot on the edge of the fire to begin to boil.

"How long you reckon 'fore the men from the ranch get here?" he asked.

Jacoby shrugged. "Who knows? If'n they left the same day Angus sent the wire, they could be here as early as tomorrow mornin', but that's unlikely. They'd have to get provisioned up and all, so I don't really 'spect them for another couple of days."

Macklin shivered as a cold wind blew up inside his jacket, and he reached for the coffeepot, which was beginning to put out some steam. "Damn," he said as he poured them both mugs of dark, strong coffee. "That means we're gonna sit out here freezin' our balls off for two or three more days."

Jacoby blew on his coffee to cool it. He glanced up at lowering, dark clouds overhead that were scurrying across the sky under heavy winds. "That's about the size of it."

Macklin shook his head, letting cigarette smoke trail from his nostrils. "I should'a taken my chances with Jensen and drawn down on him when I had the chance."

Jacoby smiled over the rim of his mug. "Then you wouldn't be out here freezing your balls off, Mac. You'd be planted forked-end-up in boot hill being food for the worms."

"Hell, maybe not. Maybe I could've taken him," Macklin argued, though it was clear from the way his face paled at the thought of bracing Jensen that he didn't believe a word of it.

"Yeah," Jacoby snorted, "an' maybe pigs can fly too."

Macklin took the cigarette out of his mouth and stared into the red-hot end for a moment. "Carl, why do you think a man like Jensen would trouble himself with a nobody like Johnny MacDougal?" He cut his eyes at Jacoby as he stuck the butt back into his mouth. "Hell, it ain't like he was gonna get more famous for killin' him."

Jacoby sipped his coffee, turning it over in his mind. "You ever think maybe Jensen didn't have no choice in the matter, Mac, that just maybe Johnny pushed the man too far and had to pay the price for it?"

"Whatta you mean?"

"Just that the men with Jensen claimed they acted in self-defense, that Johnny got pissed when one of Jensen's party beat the shit out of him, and that he drew down and fired on them first without givin' them no warning."

Macklin pursed his lips as he thought about this. "I can see it happenin', if Johnny had a snootful of liquor an' was actin' the big man like he usually did when he was drunk an' showing off in front of the boys."

He hesitated, and then he looked at Carl. "You try tellin' that little story to his sister, Sarah?"

Jacoby shook his head. "No, she wouldn't listen to anything bad about Johnny. Her and the old man both always turned a blind eye to his shortcomin's, though he certainly had plenty of 'em."

"Maybe that's why he's dead," Macklin said, flipping his butt into the coals of the fire. "If Angus would've kicked his ass a few times when he was growin' up, 'stead've lettin' him get away with being a horse's ass, maybe he'd of learned to keep his mouth shut."

Jacoby stared at Macklin. "I thought you was his best friend."

Macklin shrugged. "I was, but that don't mean I didn't see how dumb he could be sometimes. Hell, my old pappy used to take a razor strop to me if'n I got outta line, an' I soon learned to keep my mouth shut if'n I didn't have something worthwhile to say."

He yawned and got to his feet. "I'm gonna get those tents ready. Why don't you fry us up some fatback and beans so's we can eat 'fore it gets too late?"

Jacoby grinned. "I want to know who elected me the cook of this little expedition."

Macklin looked back over his shoulder as he began to unload their tents off their packhorse. "Hey, it don't make no never mind to me. You can set up the tents an' I'll cook if'n you want."

Jacoby thought about this for a moment. At least he'd be near the warm campfire if he was cooking.

"No, that's all right. You do the tents, I'll do the cooking."

Thirteen

Sarah finished with the last customer of the day and proceeded to lock up the general store. Ed and Peg Jackson had been so impressed with her work that they were now giving her almost complete authority in the running of the store when they weren't there.

Peg had grown to like her so much she'd even been hinting that if Sarah would like to attend Sunday services at their church, there were some interesting single men she would like to introduce her to.

When Sarah had finished putting the money and charge slips in the drawer behind the counter and extinguished all the lanterns, she stepped out the back door and pulled it shut behind her, turning a key in the lock. Moving quickly, she walked down the alleyway to the buckboard she'd put there in the early hours of the morning. She'd stolen the wagon from the livery stable the night before instead of just renting it. She didn't want anything pointing to her to give a posse or any of

Jensen's friends any leads on where to look for him when he turned up missing.

She climbed up onto the hurricane deck and kicked the brake with her foot, releasing it. Clicking her tongue, she whipped the twin reins against the horses' butts and urged them to get moving. It was just before five o'clock and the daylight was fading fast, and Sarah had a long way to ride — all the way out to the Sugarloaf Ranch.

She wasn't sure just how she was going to handle getting Smoke Jensen under her control, but she knew she'd figure out something. She always had in the past. Her daddy had taught her well, never telling her how to do something, just telling her what he wanted accomplished and letting her figure out the best method to get it done.

About the only thing that bothered her about what she was about to do was the thought of Sally Jensen and how it was going to affect her. She'd liked the lady from the first moment she'd met her, and Sally had been kind and considerate to her. It was a shame that Sarah was going to have to break her heart, but it couldn't be helped. Smoke Jensen was an evil man; he had to be to have done what he'd done to her brother.

As she bounced along in the buckboard, slowing as the light faded and the potholes in the road became less visible, she wondered how it was that an intelligent woman like Sally Jensen couldn't see how bad her husband was. She shook her head. She'd seen it before, women so besotted with love that they took up with men no decent lady would even talk to, much less marry or fall in love with.

She often saw these pathetic creatures when she went to town, where they walked around with heavy makeup on trying to hide the bruises the brutes they'd married seemed to give them on a regular basis.

She tried to salve her conscience by thinking how much better off Sally would be without a man like Smoke Jensen. Heck, she thought, he probably beat her when he got drunk, like a lot of those men in Pueblo did to their wives. In time, Sally would probably thank her lucky stars that he was gone.

Feeling better, Sarah turned her mind to ways that she might be able to get the drop on Jensen without any of his hands or his wife knowing she was involved. Sally knew too much about her, including the city she was from, to let her know she was involved. She needed to get the drop on Jensen and get him out to the trail without anyone from Big Rock realizing she had anything to do with it.

She slipped her hand inside the purse lying on the wooden seat next to her, and let her fingers curl over the walnut handle of the snub-nosed .38-caliber Smith and Wesson pistol that lay nestled there. Though she'd never shot anyone before, she knew she was capable of it, especially when she thought of how pale and shrunken her brother had looked in his coffin when they'd buried him out on the ranch where they'd both grown up.

Her eyes filled with tears when she pictured Johnny lying there, looking somehow smaller than he had when he was alive and being his usual obnoxious self. Angrily wiping the tears away, she leaned forward and urged the horses on, anxious to do what needed to be done.

She pulled the buckboard to a halt when she saw the lights from the Jensens' cabin through the trees. She knew from talking to Ed and Peg Jackson that the Jensens didn't have any dogs or chickens near the house to raise an alarm, so she shouldn't have any problem getting close to the house without being heard, as long as she was careful. She wasn't sure what she'd do then, but figured she'd think of something — she always did.

She climbed down off the buckboard and bent over, pulled the rear hem of her dress up between her legs, and stuck it under her belt to make the dress look like trousers. She didn't want it getting caught on any underbrush to leave traces of her having been there.

She took her pistol out of the purse, stuck it under her belt in the small of her back, and began to walk quietly toward the house in the distance, being as careful as she could not to step on any sticks or piles of leaves.

When she got to the house, she moved over under one of the windows and slowly raised her head up to peek inside. She saw Smoke and Sally talking quietly together as they ate supper at the kitchen table.

Occasionally, one or the other would smile and laugh softly at something the other said. Sarah pulled her head down and squatted under the window, wondering what she was going to do now. If worse came to worst and she didn't get another chance, she'd have to go inside the house and take them both, though she really didn't want to do that if there were any other way. Sally wasn't involved in this, and Sarah didn't want to have to scare her half to death. It'd be much better for the both of them if Jensen just disappeared and was never heard from again and Sally never found out what happened to him. That way, maybe she'd think he'd just got tired of married life and run off to live alone somewhere.

Just as she'd about resigned herself to going into the house, she heard Sally say, "I'm going to bed, dear. Are you coming?"

Sarah's heart began to beat faster when she heard Smoke reply, "Not just yet, sweetheart. I think I'll have a cigar out on the porch and another cup of coffee first."

Sarah peeked in the window and saw Sally give Smoke a quick kiss. "Good night then. I'll see you in the morning."

Smoke laughed. "Unless I wake you up when I come to bed," he joked.

"Don't you dare," Sally said with a mock frown. And then she smiled coyly and added, "Unless you plan to make it worth my while."

"Don't I always?" Smoke called as he laughed and moved out onto the front porch with a coffee cup in his hand.

Sarah waited until Smoke had finished half his cigar and most of his coffee, giving

Sally time to get to sleep, before she moved around and walked up to the porch.

When Smoke noticed her, he got to his feet, a slight frown on his face. "Why, hello, Sarah," he said, concern in his voice. "Is anything wrong?"

"Please, Mr. Jensen," Sarah said in her most helpless voice, keeping it low so as not to awaken Sally. "Come with me quickly. I need your help."

"Let me just wake Sally up," Smoke began.

"No! There's no time for that," Sarah pleaded. "Come quickly. My buckboard is just up the road a ways and I have something in it you need to see."

She turned around and moved at a fast pace down the road away from his house, not giving him time to think about it as he followed her down the dark path.

"Is someone hurt?" Smoke asked as he caught up with her and walked by her side.

"You'll see," Sarah said, avoiding the question. "It's just around the corner here."

When they came to the buckboard, Smoke leaned over the side, looking into the bed of the wagon. All he saw was a pile of blankets and some rope coiled up in the corner of the wagon. "I don't see . . ." he began, turning around to find Sarah standing a few yards away with a pistol in her hand aimed at his gut.

"What the . . . ?"

"Kindly put your hands up, Mr. Jensen," she said, her voice suddenly hard and flat.

He took a tentative step toward her and she eared back the hammer on the pistol with an audible click. "Please, Mr. Jensen, don't make me shoot you here. Just do as I say and you may live to see morning."

Smoke frowned as he raised his hands over his head.

"Now, turn around and climb into the back of the buckboard," Sarah ordered.

"Why don't you tell me what this is all about?" Smoke said as he climbed up into the bed of the wagon.

"Don't you turn around, just keep looking in that direction," Sarah ordered.

Smoke shrugged and did as she said. "Is it all right if I ask you what this is all about?" he said without turning to look at her.

Instead of answering him, Sarah reached under the seat of the buckboard and pulled out an iron crowbar she'd put there earlier. Swinging as hard as she could with one hand, she hit Smoke in the back of the head, knocking him unconscious onto his face.

She put down her gun and climbed up into the wagon with him. Taking some short lengths of rope she'd prepared earlier, she tied his hands together behind his back and then tied his feet together. Once that was done, she took some fence wire and wound it tightly around the rope, so that he couldn't possibly undo the knots she'd tied.

When she was finished, she noticed blood was pouring from a wound in the back of his head, so she took a handkerchief from her purse and tied a makeshift bandage around his head to slow the bleeding. Once it stopped, she checked to make sure he was still breathing. After all, she didn't want him to die on her — that would be too easy. She wanted him to suffer for a while, and then she wanted him to know why he was being killed before he died.

She wanted him to know that killing her brother Johnny had caused his death.

She climbed up into the seat and turned the buckboard around. She had to hurry. She wanted to be a dozen miles away before Sally Jensen woke up tomorrow morning and found her husband missing.

By the time the alarm was raised and they figured out what had happened, she should be almost home.

Moving as fast as she could over the road in the near-total blackness, Sarah took almost three hours to make her way to the outskirts of Big Rock, where she hoped to find the men from her father's ranch waiting for her along with Carl and Mac.

It'd been three full days since she'd sent Mac and Carl out to wait for them, so the men certainly should have been able to make the trip from Pueblo to here in that time.

Even looking for them and expecting to see them, Sarah almost jumped out of the heavy coat she was wearing when a dark figure materialized out of the darkness and grabbed the reins to the horses pulling the buckboard.

"Is that you, Miss Sarah?" a gruff voice called.

She took a moment to catch her breath and try to calm her racing heart. "Yes. Who are you?"

"I'm Jimmy Corbett, ma'am," the voice called back as the figure moved closer so she could make out the face.

She recognized the man then. He'd been

with her father for several years, though she didn't know him all that well personally. He was a little older than she and her brother, so Johnny had never run around with him much like he had some of the younger hands on the ranch.

"Well, Jimmy, you scared me out of two years' growth coming up on me out of the darkness like that," she complained, but her voice was level and there was no malice in it.

"Sorry, ma'am," he said, taking his hat off and standing there like a schoolboy. "Clete told us to make sure it was you 'fore we called out or anything, an' in the darkness it was kind'a hard to tell."

"That's all right, Jimmy. Where is Clete?"

Jimmy pointed up a slight rise off to her right. "He's up the top of that there hill, ma'am." He hesitated. "It's gonna be kind'a bumpy ridin' that buckboard up there. You want I should take the reins and let you ride my hoss?"

Truth to tell, Sarah's butt was aching from the long ride on the hurricane deck of the wagon, so she readily agreed. Even a saddle was better than the hard boards of the wagon seat and the continual bouncing of the wagon.

"Sure, Jimmy. Show me the way."

★ ★ ★

It didn't take long to get Cletus and the other men awake and some fresh coffee brewed. Though Sarah much preferred hot tea, she gratefully accepted a tin mug of the strong brew to help ward off the chill of the frigid night air. She hadn't realized how cold it was when she'd left town heading out to the Jensen spread, and now she was about frozen clear through.

She was about half through with her cup when Cletus finished checking out Smoke Jensen in the back of the buckboard and approached her next to the fire. Carl Jacoby was sitting next to her and Dan Macklin was on the other side. Neither had asked her how she'd managed to get Jensen in the back of the wagon, both figuring she'd tell them soon enough.

"Sarah, Jensen's more dead than alive in the back of that wagon. What'd you hit him with, an anvil?" he asked as he squatted next to her and poured himself a cup of coffee.

She cast worried eyes in the direction of the wagon. "No, just that iron crowbar under the seat."

Cletus blew on the coffee to cool it, and then took a deep swig. He glanced at her over the rim. "I'd say it's 'bout fifty-

fifty whether he makes it through the night, what with the blood he lost and the fact that he's not really dressed for this cold. The man's 'bout near froze to death."

"Sarah, didn't you think to cover him with a blanket or something?" Jacoby asked from beside her.

Angry with herself for not realizing how dangerous it would be to transport him the way she did, Sarah snapped back, "No, I didn't, Carl! It's not every day I kidnap a killer and have to drive him halfway across the country in the dead of night." She shook her head. She'd put blankets in the back of the buckboard, but those were to cover him with if anyone approached, and she simply had been too miserable with her own discomfort to think much about his.

She glanced over at the buckboard, hoping she hadn't inadvertently killed the man before she could tell him why she'd kidnapped him.

"Calm down, Sarah," Cletus said in his usual unruffled tone of voice. Sarah reflected she couldn't ever remember Cletus being riled up about anything in all the years she'd known him.

"I'm havin' a couple of the boys carry

him over here next to the fire, an' I'm gonna see if we can wake him up enough to get some hot coffee down him."

She felt her face flush with shame when she saw them carry Smoke Jensen's pale, limp body over and lay it next to the fire. Cletus was right, she thought. He does look more dead than alive.

"But Clete," she said, glancing back and forth from Smoke to him, "we've got to get moving. Come morning, his wife is going to wake up and realize he's missing. We need to be as far away when that happens as we can be."

Cletus took a deep breath and sipped more of his coffee. "Won't matter none if we kill him in the takin', Miss Sarah. If we don't get him warmed up a little an' some fluids down to replace the blood he lost, he won't make it five miles in the back of that wagon."

Just then, Smoke moaned and moved his head slightly, wincing at the pain the movement caused.

He looked around him at the campfire and the men gathered around it until his eyes landed on Sarah.

"Why?" he croaked, trying to make some sense of her attack on him.

Blushing, she got to her feet and moved

to stand over him. "Does the name Johnny MacDougal mean anything to you?" she asked, venom dripping from her voice.

Fourteen

Smoke struggled up on one elbow and looked up at the angry young woman standing over him. His head felt like a blacksmith had been pounding on it, and his eyes kept blurring and trying to cross. He concentrated, pushing the pain and nausea aside and thought about her question. The name Johnny MacDougal did stir some memories, but he couldn't quite put his finger on them just yet.

He started to shake his head in a negative reply, but he stopped when the movement caused a red-hot pain to shoot through his skull. He reached up and gingerly felt the back of his head. There was a large, squashy lump there with what felt like dried blood scabbing it over. Evidently someone, probably the very same young woman standing before him now, had hit him from behind. He'd have to get to feeling better to die, he thought.

In a hoarse voice, he croaked, "Sarah, the name is familiar to me, but I don't quite remember just why."

At her astonished glare, her eyes filled with even more hatred, he asked gently, "You want to tell me about it?"

She opened her mouth to speak, and he held up his hand, swaying slightly back and forth on his elbow as he lay there. "Just a minute, Sarah," he said, coughing. "Could I first have some water or coffee? My throat feels as dry as the desert right now."

Sarah glanced at Cletus without saying anything, and he got to his feet, poured some coffee into a tin mug, and handed it to Smoke. "Here ya go," he said, "but drink it slow so it don't come back up on ya."

While Smoke drank, Sarah put her hands on her hips and stared down at him. "For your information, Mr. Smoke Jensen, Johnny MacDougal was my brother, and last year about this time you beat him up and knocked out his teeth and then you shot him and some friends of his down in cold blood in Pueblo."

Smoke's eyes widened over the rim of the cup. He slowly lowered it and struggled up to a sitting position, trying to move his head as little as possible, his face wincing at the pain the movement caused. "That was your brother, the one dressed all in black?"

Sarah nodded, her eyes as hard as flint. Smoke let his head fall into his hands and fought back nausea the coffee had caused as he thought back about that day the previous year when William Cornelius Van Horne had offered to take Smoke and his friends to lunch. . . .

Van Horne pulled the head of his Morgan toward a dining place with a sign over the door that said simply THE FEEDBAG, and the others followed, tying their mounts and packhorses to a hitching rail in front of the building.

The Feedbag was set up similarly to Longmont's Saloon back in Big Rock. It consisted of a large room with eating tables on one side, and a bar and smaller tables for the men who just wanted to drink their meals on the other side. It was about three quarters full. Most of the men wore the canvas trousers of miners, but there was a smattering of men dressed in chaps and flannel shirts and leather vests who were obviously cowboys from nearby ranches.

Van Horne pushed through the batwings and walked directly toward a large table in the front corner of the room, while Smoke, Pearlie, Cal, and Louis spread out just inside the door with their backs to the wall waiting for their eyes to adjust to the gloomy lighting. The two mountain men stopped and eyed Smoke with raised eyebrows.

"You expectin' trouble, Smoke?" Rattlesnake Bob asked, his hand dropping to the old Walker Colt stuck in the waistband of his buckskins.

Smoke smiled as his eyes searched the room for anyone who might be giving him special attention. "No, Rattlesnake, but I've found the best way to avoid trouble is to be ready for it when it appears."

When he saw no one was looking their way, Smoke walked on over to the table where Van Horne was already sitting down talking to a waiter, and took his usual seat with his back to the wall and his face to the rest of the room.

As they all took their seats, Bill said, "I ordered us a couple of pitchers of beer to start with while we decide what to order for lunch."

Bear Tooth smacked his lips. "That sounds mighty good, Bill. I ain't had me no beer since last spring."

Before Bill could answer, a loud voice came from a group of men standing at the bar across the room. "God Almighty! What the hell is that smell?" a man called loudly, looking over at their table. "Did somebody drag a passel of skunks in here?"

The young man, who appeared to be about twenty years old, was wearing a black shirt and vest with a silver lining, and had a brace of nickel-plated Colt Peacemakers tied down low on his hips. He had four other men standing next to him, all wearing their guns in a similar manner, and all were laughing as if he'd just said something extremely funny.

Rattlesnake Bob glanced at Bear Tooth and grimaced. "I hate it when that happens," he said in a low, dangerous voice. "Now we're gonna have to kill somebody 'fore we've even had our beer."

"Take it easy, Rattlesnake," Smoke said. "He's just some young tough who's letting his whiskey do his thinking for him."

Rattlesnake eased back down in his chair. "You're right, Smoke," he said, smiling. "If'n ever' man who was drunk-dumb got kilt, there wouldn't hardly be none of us left."

Smoke continued to keep an eye on the man across the room as the bartender tried to get him to be quiet, without much success.

When their waiter appeared with the beer and glasses, Smoke asked him,

"Who's the man with the big mouth over there at the bar?"

The waiter glanced nervously over his shoulder, and then he whispered, "That's Johnny MacDougal. His father owns the biggest ranch in these parts."

"Well, I don't care if'n his daddy owns Colorado Territory," Bear Tooth growled. "You go on over there an' tell the little snot if'n he wants to see his next birthday he'd better keep his pie-hole shut."

The waiter's face paled and he shook his head rapidly back and forth. "I couldn't do that, sir," he said.

"Why not?" Rattlesnake asked.

"Just last week Johnny shot a man for stepping on his boots." The waiter hesitated, and then he added, "And the man wasn't even armed at the time."

"How come he's not in jail then?" Louis asked.

"Uh, his father carries a lot of water in Pueblo," the waiter said. "The sheriff came in and said it was in self-defense, though it was plain to everyone in the place that the man wasn't wearing a gun."

"So that's the lay of the land," Van Horne said, pursing his lips.

"Yes, sir," the waiter said, and hurried off back to the kitchen before these tough-looking men could get him in trouble, or worse yet, get him shot.

A few minutes later, after he'd downed another glass of whiskey, the young tough and his friends began to swagger across the room toward Smoke's table.

Smoke and Louis both eased their chairs back, took the hammer thongs off their Colts, and waited expectantly for the trouble they knew was coming. Smoke eased his right leg out straight under the table so he'd have quicker access if he had to draw.

MacDougal stopped a few feet behind Rattlesnake's chair and made a production of holding his nose. "Whew, something's awfully ripe in here," he said loudly, looking around the room to make sure he had an appreciative audience. "I think something done crawled in here and died."

Rattlesnake eased his hand down to the butt of the big Walker Colt in his belt, and as quick as a snake striking he whipped it out, stood up, and whirled around, slashing the young man viciously across the face with the barrel.

MacDougal screamed and grabbed his face as blood spurted onto his vest. Before the other men could react, Rattlesnake grabbed MacDougal by the hair, jerked his head back, and jammed the barrel of the gun in his mouth, knocking out his two front teeth.

As MacDougal's eyes opened wide and he moaned in pain, Rattlesnake eared back the hammer and grinned, his face inches from the young tough's. "Now, what was it you was sayin', mister?" he growled. "Somethin' 'bout somebody smelling overly ripe, I believe?"

As one of MacDougal's friends dropped his hand to his pistol, Bear Tooth stood up, and had his skinning knife against the man's throat before he could draw. "Do you really want some of this?" he asked, smiling wickedly at the man. " 'Cause if'n you do, you'll have a smile that stretches from ear to ear 'fore I'm done with you."

"Uh, no, sir!" the man said, moving his hand quickly away from his pistol butt.

MacDougal's eyes rolled back and he almost fainted from pain and embarrassment, and he sank to his knees on the floor of the restaurant.

Rattlesnake shook his head in disgust, pulled the Walker out of his bleeding mouth, and pushed him over with his boot until MacDougal was lying flat on his back, crying and moaning with his hands over his face.

Rattlesnake waved the Walker at Mac-Dougal's friends, who cringed back, and said, "You boys better take this little baby off somewheres an' get him a sugar tit to suck on 'fore he pees his pants."

The men all bent down, picked Mac-Dougal up, and helped him stagger out the batwings, their eyes fixed on the barrel of the Walker as they left.

Rattlesnake stuck the gun back in his belt and turned back to the table. "Now then, where's my beer?"

After they'd all eaten their fill of beef-steak, potatoes, corn, and apple pie for dessert, Van Horne threw some twenty-dollar gold pieces on the table and they walked toward the door.

Smoke hung back for a moment and whispered to Cal and Pearlie, who broke off from the group and exited through a side door.

He glanced at Louis and nodded. Louis nodded back and kept his hand close to the butt of his pistol. Both of them knew the trouble wasn't over yet. Men like MacDougal didn't take treatment like he'd received without trying for revenge, especially when they'd been shamed in front of their friends and neighbors.

Just before Van Horne got to the batwings, Louis and Smoke stepped in front of him. "You'd better let us go out first, Bill," Smoke said, his eyes flat and dangerous.

Smoke and Louis went through the batwings fast, Smoke breaking to the right and Louis to the left, their eyes on the street out in front of The Feedbag.

Sure enough, MacDougal and his friends were lined up in the street, pistols in their hands, cocked and ready to fire.

As they raised their hands to aim and shoot, Smoke and Louis drew, firing without seeming to aim. An instant later, Cal and Pearlie joined in from the alley where they'd come out to the side of the men in the street.

Only MacDougal, out of all the men with him, got off a shot, and it went high, taking a small piece off Smoke's hat.

The entire group of men dropped in the hail of gunfire from Smoke and Louis and the boys, sprawling in the muddy street, making it run red with their blood.

"Damn!" Rattlesnake said in awe. He had started to draw his Walker at the first sign of trouble, but it was still in his waistband by the time it was all over. "I ain't never seen nobody draw an' fire that fast," he added, glancing at Smoke and Louis with new respect.

Smoke and Louis walked out into the street and bent down to check on the men. They were all dead, or so close to dying they were no longer any risk.

A few minutes later a fat man with a tin star on his chest came running up the street. "Oh, shit!" he said when he saw who had been killed.

He looked over at Smoke and the group and moved his hand toward his pistol, until Smoke grinned and waggled his Colt's barrel at him. "I wouldn't do that, Sheriff," Smoke said, jerking his head at the group of people standing at the windows and door of The Feedbag. "There are plenty of people in there who will say we acted in self-defense, so there's no need for you to go for that hog-leg on your hip."

"But . . . but that's Angus MacDougal's son," the sheriff stammered.

Van Horne moved forward. "I don't care if it's the President's son, Sheriff. These men drew on us first."

"And just who are you?" the sheriff asked.

"My name is William Cornelius Van Horne," Bill said, pulling a card from his vest pocket and handing it to the sheriff.

"And if you'd like to send a wire to the United States marshall over in Denver, I'm sure he will vouch for me."

The sheriff eyed the men standing in front of him, and wisely decided not to make an issue of it. "All right, if it went down like you say, you're free to go." He took his hat off and wiped his forehead. "But I don't think Mr. MacDougal is gonna like this."

Rattlesnake bent over and spit a stream of tobacco juice onto Johnny MacDougal's dead face. "If'n the man has any sense, he'll be relieved that we took that sorry son of a bitch off his hands," he said. "If he'd had any sense at all, he would'a drowned him in a barrel a long time ago."

Smoke hadn't remembered Johnny Mac-Dougal's name, but he still remembered the young man's lifeless, cold eyes that barely held a hint of humanity in them as he shot off his mouth in the saloon that day. The boy was evidently spoiled rotten, and had never had to face up to the fact that people feared him because of his father's wealth, not out of any respect for him or because of any doing of his own.

He raised his eyes to Sarah's. "But his name was MacDougal and yours is . . ."

"Mine is MacDougal too," Sarah said. "I lied when I told your wife it was Johnson."

Smoke sighed and drained the last of his coffee from the cup, hoping it would stay down. "Well, if Johnny was your brother, then you know how unreasonable and stupid he was when he was drinking," Smoke said, though his gentle voice took some of the sting out of what he said.

"What?" Sarah almost screamed, stepping closer to Smoke and raising her hand as if she was about to hit him.

Smoke smiled grimly at her. "Think about it, Sarah," he said. "How many times before had he gotten drunk and caused trouble, assaulted or hurt someone? Why, the day he forced us to draw on him, I heard he'd killed an unarmed man the week before."

When Sarah's face flushed, Smoke continued. "Did anyone from your family go and tell that poor man's wife and kids you were sorry for what your brother had done, or did you just use your father's influence to sweep it all under the rug?"

"You son of a —" Sarah began.

"And did anyone from that man's family come out to the ranch and try and take Johnny prisoner or shoot him for what he'd done to their father?" he asked, his eyes boring into hers as he spoke.

"You know that was different," she almost screamed. "The man drew on Johnny first . . ." she was saying.

Smoke started to interrupt her, but his vision suddenly narrowed and everything became dark and fuzzy, and then he tipped over and fell headfirst into a deep, black pool.

Cletus rushed to his side and felt the pulse in Smoke's neck. "He's just fainted," he said, looking up at Sarah. "Probably from loss of blood, though God only knows if you've managed to scramble his brains with that crowbar."

"It'd serve the bastard right," Sarah said, moving toward the fire and the coffeepot to get herself another cup. "Especially after what he said about Johnny."

Cletus's eyes softened with sorrow, for he knew that Sarah knew that what Jensen had said was the truth, as painful as it was for her to hear it spoken out loud.

They'd all tried to maintain the fiction that the man Johnny killed had been armed, but they'd never spoken of it, and the sheriff had covered up the truth from the townspeople. But out at the ranch they'd all known how it really went down.

Fifteen

Sarah sat there, staring into the campfire over the rim of her cup, with an occasional sideways glance at Smoke. He lay still, his chest barely rising and falling, his skin as pale as the moon on a summer night. He could hardly have looked any more lifeless if he were dead.

How dare that man denigrate the memory of her brother, a man he'd callously shot down in the streets of his own town? Why, just because Johnny was a little spoiled and liked to drink and throw his weight around a little too much, that didn't mean he was a bad man. And as for that man he'd shot and killed the week before he died, her father had told her the man had a gun and that Johnny hadn't had any choice but to shoot him in self-defense.

Jensen was lying about him being unarmed; he must be, she thought as she swallowed the last of her coffee. Otherwise, the sheriff would surely have arrested Johnny. "Cletus, come here a minute, will you?" she asked as she got to her feet and moved away from the fire and the other men from the ranch.

Cletus followed her over into the darkness at the edge of camp. "Yes?"

"What Jensen said about that man Johnny shot being unarmed, that was a lie, wasn't it?" she asked, hating the whining, hopeful tone in her voice, as if she didn't really believe it herself.

Cletus pursed his lips and avoided her gaze, staring up at the stars while debating within himself how to answer her question. On the one hand, he wanted to tell her the truth, but on the other, Angus had sworn him to secrecy.

Sarah was no fool. She heard him hesitate and saw the pain in his eyes when he turned them back to her. "Oh, Clete," she said before he could answer. "Why didn't Daddy tell me the truth?"

He shrugged, glad he hadn't had to lie to her after all. "I don't know, Missy," he said, using the pet name he'd given her when she was just a toddler. "I suppose he felt it was best that you didn't know."

She looked over her shoulder at Jensen, who still hadn't moved. "Then he was right about Johnny, wasn't he?" she asked, her voice low and sad.

Cletus put his hand on her shoulder. "Now, Missy, just because Johnny was a little rough around the edges sometimes didn't give anyone the right to shoot him down in cold blood, no matter how drunk he was or what he may have said to them."

Sarah nodded distractedly, but she was thinking, What if Johnny did more than just shoot his mouth off? What if he'd drawn on Jensen and his men as Jensen maintained he did? What would she do then? Could she stand to take this man to her father where he would be killed if he were in fact innocent of any wrongdoing?

She moved over closer to the fire, chilled by more than the freezing air around her. She had some tough decisions to make, and for once, she wouldn't have her father to guide her in the making of them. Somehow, before they arrived back at the ranch, she would have to decide just who was telling the truth about what had happened last year in the streets of Pueblo.

She turned to Cletus. "We'd better get a move on, Clete," she said. "Jensen's wife is going to wake up before too long, and then we're going to have a posse to deal with if we're not a lot of miles away from here."

Cletus looked over at Jensen, whose chest was rising and falling rapidly with shallow breaths. "I don't know, Missy. If we move him now, he's liable to start to bleedin' inside his head or something." He turned back to her. "Angus ain't gonna like it if'n we bring him back a corpse."

She turned to face him, putting her hands on her hips and looking him right in the eye. "He also won't like it much if his only daughter is arrested and hung for kidnapping, Clete. Now, either we get a move on and Jensen takes his chances, or we shoot him here and leave him for the buzzards to find."

Cletus shook his head and spit out, "Damn, but you're just like your old man — headstrong and stubborn as a mule!"

Sarah smiled and reached up to pat Cletus's cheek, something a man would have gotten shot trying. "I take that as a compliment, Clete. Now, get a move on . . . please."

Three hours later, just as the sun was edging over mountain peaks to the east, Smoke rolled over in the back of the buckboard and got up on his hands and knees. His head hung down, and he vomited until he thought he was going to bring up his toes.

Cletus, who was riding on the hurricane

deck, looked back over his shoulder and grimaced at the nasty sight. "Shit," he said, "now you're gonna have to ride in that the rest of the way home."

Smoke glared up at him, his face pasty and pale, his eyes sunken and surrounded by black. Suddenly, his lips curled in a smile that made the hair on the back of Cletus's neck stand up. He'd never seen anything as dangerous in his life.

"What're you grinnin' at, Jensen?" Cletus asked. "It 'pears to me like you got precious little to smile at."

"Mister," Smoke croaked through dry and cracked lips, "I was just thinking about how good it is gonna feel when I make all of you pay for this." He coughed and leaned his head to the side as he spit out a clot of old blood. "Ordinarily, I get no pleasure from killing men, but for this group, I'm gonna have to make an exception."

"Only one's gonna get kilt around here is you, Jensen," Cletus said before he turned back around to face the horses before Jensen could see the fear in his eyes — eyes that had never been made to show fear before.

"Better men than you and these mangy coyotes riding with you have tried to plant

183

me forked-end-up, mister," Smoke said as he struggled to get turned around so he could put his back to the sideboard of the wagon. After a moment, he succeeded, and he leaned there with his elbows on his knees. "And I'm still kicking," Smoke added after a moment spent getting his breath from the exertion his moving had caused.

Sarah gently spurred Cletus's horse she was riding, and pulled the animal up next to the bed of the wagon where Smoke sat with his back to her.

Neither Cletus nor Smoke could see her as Cletus called back over his shoulder, "Yeah, but you ain't never killed no MacDougal before neither, Jensen."

Smoke snorted. "If you're talking about that man named Johnny I shot in Pueblo last year, the only thing special about him was his capacity to drink enough liquor to make him both stupid and dangerous."

Cletus nodded, his attention on the horses in front of him. "Yeah, Johnny could put the tonsil paint away, all right. But that didn't give you no right to beat him near half to death an' then shoot him full'a lead."

Smoke sighed. "What's wrong with you people?" he asked, his voice low as if he were talking to himself, exasperated at their unwillingness to learn the truth. "Didn't anybody ask the sheriff what had happened? There were plenty of witnesses to the whole thing."

"All we heard was that Johnny got pistol-whipped and all his teeth were knocked out, and then he and his friends got shot down without being able to get off any shots themselves." Cletus looked back over his shoulder again. "That don't exactly sound like no fair fight to me, Jensen."

Smoke held his head. All this talking was making his head feel as if it was going to explode. What was it about self-defense that these people didn't understand? Surely they must have known what kind of a man Johnny was.

"I'll try one more time, then I'm done talking," Smoke said. "Johnny had a snootful of liquor and came over to our table and braced the men I was with, saying they stunk like skunks and garbage. Well, it's no surprise that one of the mountain men I was with took offense at his remarks and proceeded to beat the shit out of him, which he no doubt deserved. After Johnny got knocked flat on his back, his friends came over and carried him outside. Later, after we'd finished our supper, we walked out the door. Johnny and all his friends were standing there in the street with their hands filled with iron — we had no choice but to shoot."

Cletus turned his head. "You that good, Jensen, you can draw and kill a man who's already got his pistol out?"

Smoke chuckled. "Why don't you try me, mister, and find out for yourself, or do you let a mob do your fighting for you? You got the balls for it, give me a gun and we'll see if I'm fast enough to take the lot of you."

Cletus gritted his teeth and looked ahead. A lot of what the man said made sense. He'd loved Johnny like his own son, but that didn't mean the little bastard wasn't mad-dog mean when he'd been drinking. He shook his head. It could well have gone down just like Jensen said, but if it did, why didn't Sheriff Tupper tell it that way to Angus?

Sarah, who was wondering the same thing, flicked her riding crop at Smoke and got his attention. When he turned his head to look at her riding alongside the wagon, she said, "That isn't exactly the way the sheriff tells it, Mr. Jensen, and why would he lie about it?"

Smoke smirked and turned back around,

speaking over his shoulder. "Your father has a reputation of not listening to people who tell him what he doesn't want to hear, Sarah. My guess is, the sheriff was too scared to tell him his little boy got killed because he got drunk and let his mouth override his butt. Truth be told, Johnny wasn't near as tough or as fast with a gun as the liquor made him think he was, and he seemed too busy showing off for all of his friends to think straight about it."

Sarah swiped at the back of Smoke's head with her crop. "You bastard!" she yelled, and spurred her horse into a full gallop, riding off in a cloud of dust.

Cletus shook his head as he watched Sarah gallop off up ahead of the column of men. "Boy, you sure know how to end a conversation."

"I guess her father's not the only one doesn't like to be told the truth, especially when her mind's already made up on the subject."

Sixteen

Sally woke up just as the sun was coming up and brightening the bedroom. She yawned and, as she did every morning, stuck out her right hand and felt around the bed for her husband. When she didn't feel Smoke next to her, she opened her eyes and rolled on her side. His side of the bed was smooth, and his pillow was unwrinkled.

She sat up straight, rubbing sleep out of her eyes. Evidently, he hadn't come to bed last night, because she'd never known him to get up early and make his side of the bed while she was still sleeping.

Something was wrong.

She jumped out of bed and got dressed. As she was heading for the door, she noticed that Smoke's hat and guns were hanging on the peg next to the front door. He would never have gone anywhere without them.

She crossed the porch and ran to the bunkhouse. She pounded on the door until Cal opened it, yawning widely. It was just about time for the cowboys to rise, but it was evident he hadn't had his morning coffee just yet.

"Oh, hi, Miss Sally," he said, his voice still husky from sleep.

"Cal, have any of you seen Smoke this morning?"

"Uh, why, no, Miss Sally. We just got up an' ain't seen nobody yet."

"Damn!" she said, thinking furiously. "Did you see or hear anything out of the ordinary last night?"

Cal shook his head, his expression changing to one of alarm at her questions.

Without saying anything else, she turned back toward the barn and took off at a dead run. She wanted to go and see if Smoke's horse was still there, though she knew he'd never have gotten on his horse and left without saying something to her, or at least grabbing his hat and guns from the cabin.

Cal glanced over his shoulder and called out, "Pearlie, somethin's wrong. Get on out here." Then he took off at a run after Sally, tucking in his shirt on the go.

Twenty minutes later, the three of them sat at the kitchen table in the ranch house. Sally had put some coffee on to boil while she told them about Smoke's mysterious absence.

"And he didn't say nothin' 'bout goin' nowheres when you went to bed last night?" Pearlie asked as she handed him a steaming cup.

She shrugged and shook her head. "No. He went out on the porch to have a cigar and a cup of coffee before he came to bed, and he said he'd see me in a while."

"It ain't like Smoke to just take off without tellin' nobody," Cal said, getting up from his chair. "Especially if there was trouble brewin'."

He moved out onto the front porch and began to look around, even getting down on his knees to get a better look at the ground around the porch.

"Look here," he said to Sally and Pearlie, who were standing behind him. He pointed to a half-smoked cigar lying on the ground next to the porch, and a cup that still held a third of a cup of cold coffee in it on the arm of a wooden chair.

"Looks like somethin' spooked him, or at least made him throw down his cigar and leave his coffee 'fore he was through with either one," Cal said.

"You see any tracks, Cal?" Pearlie asked, moving over to lean over his shoulder. Cal was smart and quick, but Pearlie was the more experienced tracker by far.

"Yeah. Most of 'em head over toward the bunkhouse," Cal replied, "but it looks like two sets go off down the road that'a way. And see, one set looks smaller, like it might'a been a woman, or maybe a boy."

Pearlie bent down and gently fingered the tracks. "You're right, Cal, and these are from last night too."

"How can you tell that?" Cal asked.

"Here, see how the other tracks are crusted over where they've been wet by dew that's dried a few times?"

When Cal nodded, Pearlie added, "Well, these here fresh tracks are still soft and damp, so they've only had the dew fall on them once and they haven't dried yet, so they must've been made last night."

"Pearlie," Sally said, reaching inside the door and pulling a gun from Smoke's holster, "follow the tracks and show us where they lead."

Pearlie followed the tracks, walking bent over like an old man as the tracks led him down the road away from the Jensens' cabin. Finally, he stopped and pointed. "Look there, Miss Sally. Tracks of a buckboard right here where these two sets stop."

"Shoot!" Sally said. "That's not much help. Everyone in the valley has a buckboard."

"Yeah," Cal added. "An' followin' those buckboard tracks once they get on the main road will be impossible."

Pearlie, who was still staring at the tracks, shook his head. "Maybe, but these tracks show the iron on the wheels to be brand-new. Lookit how sharp the edges of the tracks are. They ain't worn at all." He looked up at Sally and Cal, who weren't following him. "Don't you see?" he asked. "All we have to do is ask Jed the blacksmith who's had their wheels re-ironed lately and we'll know who was here."

Sally grabbed Pearlie and hugged him, causing him to blush furiously. "Pearlie, you're a genius," she said, and she turned and ran back toward the cabin.

By the time they got to Big Rock, it was almost nine o'clock in the morning, and they rode directly to Jed Blankenship's blacksmith shop.

"Oh, no," Sally said when she dismounted and walked up to the door. There was a sign on it that was too small for the boys to read from their horses.

"What's it say, Miss Sally?" Cal asked.

"Jed's not here. He's gone to Silver City to help his brother who broke his leg. He won't be back for at least a week."

"You want me to hightail it over to Silver City and see what he has to say?" Pearlie asked.

Sally thought about it for a moment. "No, it'll probably be quicker just to divide up the ranches around town and all of us ride around asking whose buckboard it might be."

"Maybe it's something simple, like one of your neighbors came by last night askin' Smoke for help," Cal observed.

Sally shook her head. "No. If that were the case, Smoke would still have had time to either wake me up or to get his hat and guns from the rack next to the door. You know he never leaves the house without them."

Both Cal and Pearlie nodded. "That's right, Miss Sally. An' if'n one of the neighbors needed Smoke's help, he would've asked either you or Cal or me to come along," Pearlie said.

"Yes, so I suspect Smoke is in some kind of trouble, and it's up to us to figure out who took him and then to make sure we get him back."

"You know, it might be kind'a dangerous for you to go ridin' up to the ranches askin' 'bout where Smoke is," Pearlie advised. "If'n they took him an' you show up, you're liable to get shot."

Sally smiled grimly and patted the snub-nosed .36-caliber Smith and Wesson revolver on her hip. "It won't be dangerous for me, boys. It'll be dangerous for whoever took Smoke."

"Speakin' of that," Cal said, "why don't we ask Monte and Louis to help us look for him? That'd sure cut down the time it's gonna take to find that buckboard."

"Hell, they might even know whose it is," Pearlie added.

"Good idea, Cal. Let's ride on over to Longmont's and see who's in there."

Sally sent Pearlie to the sheriff's office while she and Cal walked directly to Longmont's Saloon. As much a café as a drinking and gambling establishment, the place was half-full of patrons eating one of Chef Andre's magnificent breakfasts.

Louis was, as usual, sitting at his private table drinking strong coffee and smoking a thin, black cheroot. When he saw Sally and Cal, he immediately put the cigar out and got to his feet, motioning them over to his table.

He gave a very slight bow. "Good morning, Sally, Cal."

He pulled a chair out and as Sally took a

seat, he asked, "Will Smoke be joining us this morning?"

She shook her head, and he noticed her eyes were wet with unshed tears. "No, Louis, but Pearlie will be here shortly with Sheriff Carson."

Louis sat down, glancing at Cal for some clue as to what was going on.

"Smoke seems to have disappeared sometime last night, Louis," Cal said.

Louis held up four fingers to the young black waiter without taking his eyes off Sally. "Do you have any idea what happened?" he asked while the waiter put four coffee mugs on the table and began to pour them all coffee.

She shook her head. "No. Everything was normal when I went to bed last night. Smoke said he was going to have a cigar and a cup of coffee on the porch and he would be right in." She took a moment to wipe daintily at her eyes with a handkerchief, and then she continued. "I fell asleep, and woke up this morning and he was nowhere to be found."

Just then Monte Carson, sheriff of Big Rock, joined them along with Pearlie.

"Pearlie's told me the gist of things, Sally," he said. "Are you sure Smoke didn't leave of his own accord, maybe 'cause this

195

woman or boy came by needin' help?"

She shook her head. "No, Monte. His guns and his hat were still on the peg next to the door."

Monte glanced at Louis. They both knew Smoke would no more leave his house without his hat and guns than he would walk down Main Street naked. There were just too many men roaming around the country who'd like nothing better than to catch Smoke Jensen unarmed and defenseless.

Monte nodded. "You're right, Sally. I'm sure foul play's involved here."

"Sheriff, we found some tracks of a buckboard with new iron rims on the wheels. The tracks make it look like Smoke went off in the buckboard," Pearlie said.

"New rims, huh?" Monte said, stroking his jaw before picking up his mug and drinking some coffee. "Guess I'd better go on over to Jed's and see who's had new rims put on lately."

"Won't do, Monte," Cal said. "We've been there. Jed's out of town for a few days on over to Silver City."

"He at his brother's place?" Monte asked.

When Sally and the boys nodded, Monte got to his feet. "I'll go by the telegraph office and send a wire to the sheriff there askin' him to take a ride out to Jed's brother's place and see if he can find out what we need to know."

Louis nodded. "Meanwhile, we can split up and ride out to some of the nearby ranches and take a look at their wagons."

Monte scratched his jaw again. "I don't know if that's such a good idea, Louis," he said in his slow drawl. "If'n Smoke was took against his will, whoever took him ain't gonna welcome any questions with open arms."

Louis frowned. "You're right, Monte. We'd need to go in posse strength at least since we don't know how many men we're dealing with here."

Monte took his ever-present pipe out of his shirt pocket and began filling it with sweet-smelling tobacco from a leather pouch. "Why don't you all just sit here and have some breakfast? It shouldn't take more'n a couple of hours to get an answer from the sheriff over at Silver City. Then we can all go together to find out just what's goin' on."

Sally looked up at him. "I don't know if I can just sit here without doing something, Monte, not while Smoke is in danger."

Monte patted her shoulder as clouds of

blue smoke whirled from his pipe. "I know it's tough, Sally, but you won't be doing him any good if you go out and get caught by the same people."

"You're correct, Monte. I'm being foolish."

"No, you're not," Louis said, waving his hand at the waiter to come and take their orders. "You're just being a wife who's worried about her man. Nothing wrong with that."

"You know, Sheriff," Pearlie said, scratching his head. "I just don't hardly think it's anybody from around here took Smoke. Hell, ever'body that lives within fifty miles of Big Rock is good friends with Smoke and Sally."

Monte nodded. "You're probably right, Pearlie. But there ain't been no suspicious strangers hanging around town for the past couple of weeks, and we got to start looking somewhere."

Sally nodded. "You're right, Monte. Why don't you go on over to the telegraph office while we have some breakfast?"

Seventeen

As they rode down the trail toward Pueblo and home, Sarah MacDougal struggled with her conscience. The more she was around Smoke Jensen, the less he seemed like a crazed gunfighter out to kill anyone who got in his way and the more he seemed like an honest, decent human being.

She thought back to when Sheriff Tupper had come to give her and her father the news of Johnny's death. As she went over what he'd said on that visit, she realized that she and her father hadn't really heard what he was trying to say.

He'd tried to tell them, in his own mealymouthed way, that it was Johnny's fault he'd been shot. Of course, neither she nor her father had been willing to listen to that explanation, not when their kin was lying dead in the back of Tupper's wagon, his teeth knocked out and his body full of a stranger's lead.

"Missy," Cletus called from the seat of the buckboard alongside her.

"Yes?"

"I think it's time we took a noonin' an' rested our mounts. We keep goin' at this pace, we're gonna lose a couple of 'em 'fore too long." He grinned. "An' I don't hanker to carry none of these boys on my back."

"All right," she agreed, pointing to a copse of trees off to the right about a hundred yards ahead. "Pull over there and we'll fix up some grub for the men and give the horses some grain and water."

She glanced down sideways at Smoke, who was riding in the back of the wagon. "Jensen, don't you go getting any ideas about trying to make a break for it. My father wants you brought back alive, but he won't quibble if you're killed trying to escape."

Smoke shrugged. "This is your party, Sarah. I'm just along for the ride." He gingerly felt the large knot on the back of his head. "Besides, if I tried to run right now, I think my head would fall off."

"You keep thinking like that and you may just survive this trip," she said, blushing a little at his mention of the damage she'd done to his head.

He glanced up at her and smiled, no fear at all evident in his eyes. "What about the homecoming?" he asked. "Will I survive that too?"

Sarah's face flushed even more, and she spurred her horse on up ahead to tell the men to ready the camp without trying to give him an answer.

While Cletus oversaw the cooking of fatback and beans and the heating of coffee, Sarah walked over to stand next to Smoke, who was sitting with his back to a tree while two men held pistols on him from a short distance away.

"You understand why I'm doing this, don't you, Mr. Jensen?" she asked.

He glanced up at her. "Of course I do, Sarah. You've lost a brother, and your father has lost a son. Neither one of you wants to admit to yourselves that it might have been your fault for not making him grow up better, so you're planning on taking it out on me." He smiled, though there was no mockery in his expression. "It's simple when you think about it. I'm to be a scapegoat for your dad's failure as a parent and your failure as a sister."

She flushed, angered by the way he was continually turning things around and trying to shift the blame to anyone but himself. "That's not true. I'm taking you back because you must be punished for what you did."

"Punished for defending myself?" he asked, the grin still on his face. "For doing what the law should have done a long time ago when your brother killed his first man?"

"Oh, you're just impossible," Sarah said, stamping her foot and walking quickly over to stand next to Cletus at the campfire.

"It's not easy being judge, jury, and executioner, Sarah," Smoke called to her back. "I don't think you're going to like the job much."

Cletus glanced up at her as he poured her a cup of coffee and handed it to her, noticing the redness of her eyes and her hunched-over shoulders and stiff neck. "He getting your goat, Missy?" he asked gently.

"Yes," she said, taking the cup and blowing on it to cool it down enough to drink. "He twists everything around so you'd think he should get a medal for shooting Johnny, instead of . . ." She paused, not wanting to put into words what was waiting for Smoke at her father's ranch.

"Instead of being killed in cold blood by your daddy or you?" Cletus asked, getting to his feet.

"I didn't say that!"

He shook his head. "No, but you know that's what's gonna happen, don't you?" he asked. "You're not fooling yourself into thinking anything different, are you?"

She hung her head. "I . . . I guess I know what's going to happen," she finally answered, her voice low.

"Good," he said. " 'Cause if you're gonna do this, you better be able to live with it, or it'll eat you alive. You'd better figure you're right and it needs doin'. Otherwise, well, otherwise maybe you ought to ride on ahead and let me take him the rest of the way."

"Don't treat me like a baby, Clete."

"I'm not, Missy. But I can see by lookin' in your eyes you got some doubts 'bout all this." He sighed as he drank his coffee. "I've known men out on the trail did something that got one of their friends killed. Most of 'em knew it comes with the job of cowboying, but a few never got over it. Their lives were plumb ruined by one little mistake that could've happened to anybody." He stared hard at her. "I don't want that to happen to you, Missy."

"Yes, I do have some doubts, Clete," she admitted. "What if what he says happened is the true story? What if he had no choice but to shoot Johnny in self-defense?"

Cletus shrugged. "What really happened don't make no never mind to me," he said. "I take my orders from your daddy, an' he said to bring this man to him. Far as what happens then, it ain't no concern of mine."

"So, you won't feel responsible when Daddy shoots this man you're taking to him?"

Cletus looked surprised. "Responsible? Hell, no, not unless I pull the trigger myself."

"And would you do that, if my father told you to?" she asked, peering at him over the rim of her mug as she drank.

He looked down at his feet. "I don't know, Missy, I just don't know."

"I'm ashamed of us both, Clete. You for not being man enough to take responsibility for what you're doing, and me for not finding out the truth about what happened before taking Jensen prisoner."

After they'd eaten and fed the horses, Cletus called three men over to him. "Bob, you and Billy and Juan head on back down our back trail. Take your rifles and plenty of ammunition along with you. Anybody comes up the trail looks like they following us, you slow 'em down."

"What if'n it's a big posse, Clete?" Bob Bartlett asked.

Cletus looked around at the rising ground on either side of the trail. "There's plenty of places along here where you boys can get the high ground, Bob. You do that and you ought'a be able to hold the trail against a dozen men or more if'n you have to."

"You want we should kill them, Jefe?" Juan Gomez asked, grinning like that was something he wouldn't mind doing at all.

Cletus shook his head. "Not unless you absolutely have to, boys. Just shoot close enough to make them think twice about following us. I don't want to start a war here by killin' some lawmen and deputies, not unless there's no other way."

"But Boss," Billy Free said, "if there is no other way, then what should we do?"

Cletus shrugged. "Try for the horses first, the men last, but keep them off our backs until we get to the ranch. Understand?"

Several hours later, longer than the "couple of hours" Monte had promised, Jimmy from the telegraph office came running into Longmont's, where the group was gathered impatiently waiting for word

205

from the blacksmith.

They'd all drunk so much coffee they felt as if they were floating, and even Andre's sumptuous breakfasts hadn't done much to cheer them up.

Jimmy handed the wire to the sheriff, who thanked him and slowly unfolded the yellow foolscap paper. He snorted when he read it, and got to his feet.

"Damn, I should'a knowed as much," he said, a wry look on his face.

"What does it say, Monte?" Sally asked, also getting to her feet.

"Jed says the only new rim he's put on in the last month was for the livery rental wagon."

Louis snapped his fingers. "Of course. We should have known that Pearlie was right and that no one who lived around here would be a party to any action against Smoke. It had to be an outsider."

"But Monte," Sally asked, a puzzled look on her face. "Why would someone be so dumb as to come into town and rent a wagon to kidnap someone as well known as Smoke is?" She shook her head. "That would leave a trail pointing straight back to them as soon as we talked to the livery agent."

"Sally," Monte said, "when you've been

206

a sheriff as long as I have, you'll soon learn that most men who ride the owlhoot trail are as dumb as a post." He chuckled as he settled his hat on his head. "Hell, if'n they was smart, they'd get a job as sheriff like me an' get rich."

They all laughed nervously as they hurried down the street toward the livery stable.

Fred Morgan shook his head when they asked him who had recently rented his wagon with the new iron rim on the wheels. "Can't rightly say, Sheriff," he drawled in his backwoods accent, a long piece of straw hanging from the corner of his mouth that bobbed up and down as he chewed the wad of tobacco stuck in his cheek.

Monte sighed. Sometimes, talking to Fred was like pulling teeth. It took a lot of effort, and the results were usually less than satisfying. "Why not, Fred?" he asked, trying to be patient.

Fred shrugged. "Why, 'cause nobody *rented* the buckboard, Sheriff. They stole it night 'fore last."

Monte cocked his head and put his hands on his hips. "You mean someone took the wagon without paying you for it?"

"That's right."

"Well, why in hell didn't you report it to me?" Monte asked, getting red in the face.

Morgan held up his hands to calm the sheriff. " 'Cause it happens all the time, Sheriff. Lots of times folks will find they need a wagon in the middle of the night 'cause theirs broke down, so instead of waking me up, they just take one of mine. Heck-fire, they always bring 'em back in a day or two."

Monte smirked. "I think this time your wagon is gone for good, Fred."

"But who round here'd do something mean like that?" Fred asked in a whining voice.

"They probably weren't from around here, Mr. Morgan," Sally said, her voice sad.

As they walked slowly back to Longmont's, she asked, "Monte, what do you think we ought to do now? That wagon with the new rim was our only clue as to who may have taken Smoke."

Monte pursed his lips. "Well, there's only four ways they could have gone, so I guess the best thing to do is send riders out along each of the trails leading from town. Sooner or later, they've got to come across those wagon tracks."

"And until they do?" Sally asked.

"I'd suggest you go on back to the Sugarloaf and get packed up for a trip," Monte said. "Soon as the men find out which way they've gone, we'll get a posse together and go after them."

Sally thought about this for a moment, and then she shook her head. "No, Monte, I don't think that's a very good idea."

"And why not, Sally?"

"A large posse would be too easy to spot, and it would move too slow. I think just five or six men should be enough." She glanced around at Louis, who smiled and nodded his head. "I think Cal and Pearlie, Louis and you, and of course me will be more than enough."

"But Sally," Monte argued. "We don't even know how many men we'll be going up against nor which way they went."

She smiled. "Monte, outside of Smoke himself, you four men are the best men I know to have on my side in a fight. No matter what the odds are, I think the five of us will be able to handle it, and from what I hear, Pearlie can track a mouse in a blizzard. We should be all right."

Monte nodded, his lips tight. "I hope you're right, Sally."

Eighteen

The next morning, with their saddlebags packed for a long trip, Sally and Cal and Pearlie rode back into Big Rock. As they were passing the general store, Peg Jackson stepped out on the boardwalk in front and waved to Sally.

"Sally, can I talk to you for a minute?" she called.

"Why don't you boys go on over to Longmont's while I have a few words with Mrs. Jackson?" she said.

Cal and Pearlie tipped their hats to Peg and rode off down the street. Sally climbed down off her horse, tied it to the hitching rail, and then turned to Peg.

"Yes, Peg?"

"I was just wondering if you'd seen Sarah Johnson in the last couple of days," Peg said.

Sally thought back. "Why, no. In fact the last time I saw her was the last time I was in your store."

"That's strange," Peg said, looking worried. "I really don't believe she has any other friends in town she might be staying with."

"What do you mean?" Sally asked. "Is she missing?"

"Oh, I don't know as I'd go that far," Peg answered. "It's just that she hasn't been to work for the past couple of days, and she didn't tell me she wasn't going to come in."

Sally shrugged. "Maybe she quit, or got a better job."

"I don't think so," Peg said. "I still owe her for three days' work. If she was quitting, don't you think she'd come by for her money?"

"Yes, I do," Sally said. "Have you checked with her landlady?"

"No, not yet," Peg said. "I just assumed she was sick or under the weather or something."

"Well, she's been staying at Mamma Rogers' place. I can go by there on my way to Longmont's," Sally said. "I'll just stick my head in and see if she's all right."

"Oh, thank you, Sally. That would put my mind at ease," Peg said. "After all, she's such a nice young woman."

Mamma Rogers opened the door and smiled at Sally. "Oh, howdy, Sally," she said. "Come on in."

As Sally entered the parlor, she asked, "Melissa, is Sarah Johnson in her room? I'd like to talk to her."

Rogers frowned. "Funny you should mention that," she said. "I think she moved out."

"Why is that?" Sally asked.

"Well, I didn't see or hear her for a couple of days, so I peeked into her room. The bed hadn't been slept in and all of her clothes were gone."

"Did she leave owing you rent?"

"Oh, no. Matter of fact, she's paid up through next week. It is kind'a funny, though, that she didn't ask for a refund if she was leaving for good."

Sally began to get an itch at the back of her neck that told her something was wrong. She remembered the smaller set of tracks they'd found along with Smoke's. "Did Sarah have any callers while she was here?" she asked.

Rogers frowned. "Well, you know I don't allow gentlemen visitors to my women boarders, but a couple of times two men did stop by and leave messages for her."

"Citizens of Big Rock?"

Rogers shook her head. "No, they were strangers. Far as I know, they were staying over at the hotel on Main Street."

"Strangers, huh?" Sally asked.

"Yeah, and come to think of it, I haven't see the two of them the past few days either."

"Maybe I'll just stop by the hotel and see what's going on," Sally said.

The desk clerk smiled at Sally as he flipped through the pages of his register book. "Oh, here it is, Missus Jensen. Their names were Carl Jacoby and Daniel Macklin. Macklin's been here a few months. Jacoby arrived not too long ago."

"Could I see that book, Mort?" she asked.

"Certainly," he said, turning it around so she could read the names.

It was just as she'd suspected. Both men had signed a home address of Pueblo, Colorado.

"Thank you, Mort," she said as she turned and rushed out the door toward Longmont's.

As she approached the table where Louis and Monte Carson and the boys were sitting, the sheriff stood up. "I'm sorry, Sally, but the boys haven't been able to find those wagon tracks yet."

"I think we need to look along the trail that goes toward Pueblo, Monte."

"What? Why do you say that?" he asked.

Sally shook her head and sat down. "I don't know exactly, but there are some very strange things happening that concern a young lady that is from there."

She went on to tell them all she'd found out before coming to the saloon.

She noticed Cal and Pearlie looking at each other, and sighed when Pearlie nudged Louis with his elbow.

"All right, men," she said. "Just what is going on?"

"Uh, Sally," Louis began, "Pearlie just reminded me of something that happened when we went through Pueblo on the way up to Canada last year."

"Uh-huh?"

"There was a gunfight and some men from Pueblo were killed by our group."

"Any of them named Johnson, or Jacoby, or Macklin?" she asked, her stomach doing flip-flops.

"No, not as I recall," Louis said.

Sally glanced at Monte, who was sitting next to her. "Monte, I think Smoke's disappearance ties in somehow with that of the girl who called herself Sarah Johnson. Now that I think about it, she was awfully curious about Smoke when we met on the train. I didn't catch it at the time, but she asked a lot of questions about him."

"And you think that ties in with the killing in Pueblo last year?" he asked.

She shrugged. "Probably, but it doesn't matter. We have four people who've disappeared from Big Rock in the last few days, so there's got to be some connection."

"She's right, Monte," Louis said. "What are the odds of that happening and it not being related?"

Monte got up from the table. "I agree. Let's get moving up the trail to Pueblo."

"I'll bet you a dollar against one of Miss Sally's bear sign we find those buckboard tracks 'fore we go ten miles," Pearlie said to Cal as he got to his feet and set his hat low on his head.

"I won't bet, but I hope you're right," Cal replied, following him toward the door.

Meanwhile, Cletus and Sarah and their men were getting closer to Pueblo, where Angus MacDougal had some plans for Smoke Jensen.

Sarah was beginning to feel less and less sure that she was doing the right thing. The more she talked to Smoke, the harder

215

it was for her to see him as a cold-blooded killer. In spite of how she'd tricked and betrayed him in order to take him to her father, he seemed to bear her no malice. When she asked him about this, he just shrugged. "I guess I'd probably feel much the same way if I were in your shoes," he told her. "Matter of fact," he added, thinking of the time he'd gone after the men who'd raped his wife and killed her and his son, "I have done pretty much the same thing — the only difference was, I knew I was right and you don't."

That night they stopped and fixed camp for the last time. By the end of the next day, Cletus said they'd be at the MacDougal ranch.

Exhausted from the ride and her mental battle with herself about the rightness of what she'd done, Sarah flopped down on the ground near the fire and stared into the flames, as if she could find some answers there.

Smoke, who was standing a few yards away with his hands tied, glanced her way. His eyes widened and he took two quick steps and launched himself at her headfirst.

His body slammed into hers, knocking her to the side and almost into the flames.

Cletus, seeing this and hearing Sarah's cry of surprise and pain, whipped out his Walker Colt and aimed it at the back of Smoke's head.

Before he could pull the trigger, he saw Smoke twist his body around and lift his boots into the air. A dark brown, mottled shape flashed into the light and a five-foot long timber rattler struck at Smoke's boots, its fangs slashing a double groove in the soles of the shoes.

"Damn!" Jimmy Corbett yelled as he jumped to the side to get out of the way of the angry critter.

Smoke brought the heels of his boots down hard, smashing the snake in the head and dazing it.

Cletus, finally seeing what was going on, stepped over and put a bullet between the snake's eyes, blowing its head off.

"What . . . why . . . ?" a startled Sarah cried from where she lay, a few feet away.

Cletus holstered his pistol and moved to her side, helping her to her feet. She leaned over Smoke, looked at the dead snake, and shuddered.

"You saved my life," she murmured.

"Naw, probably not," Smoke said, struggling to sit up, the task difficult with his hands still tied behind his back. "The poor critter was just trying to get to the fire to warm himself up a bit. When it's this cold outside, they can't move very fast."

Cletus snorted. "Hell, boy," he said. "He didn't look all that slow when he struck at your boots."

Smoke just shrugged. "Now that the excitement is over, how about a cup of that coffee that's boiling over by the fire?" he asked.

Cletus nodded, and moved over to squat next to the pot and pour a mug. He looked at Sarah, who was standing next to him. "You're right, Missy," he said in a low voice so only she could hear him. "That boy did save your life, and at some risk to his own."

"I know," she said, squatting next to Cletus and holding out her mug for some of the steaming brew.

Cletus glanced over his shoulder at Smoke. "You know, Missy," he said, "this is the first time in more'n twenty years I been workin' for your daddy that I feel like he's dead wrong 'bout somethin'."

"What are we going to do, Clete?" she asked, holding the mug in both hands to warm them up.

"I don't know, Missy," he said, his voice heavy and sad. "I'm afraid we've both got some thinkin' to do on it 'fore we get home tomorrow."

He got slowly to his feet, and carried the mug of coffee over and handed it to Smoke, who nodded his thanks.

"Uh . . . I want to thank you for what you done, Jensen," Cletus said, the words coming hard.

Smoke eyed him. "Sarah means something special to you, doesn't she, Cletus?" Smoke asked.

"I'm her godfather, and I've knowed her all her life," Cletus answered.

Smoke nodded slowly, sipping the coffee. "Then, you're welcome, Cletus."

Later that night, after everyone had eaten and while even the sentries were dozing in their appointed spots, Sarah slipped out of her blankets and crawled over to where Smoke lay curled up next to the coals of the fire.

Sometime in the last couple of hours, the lowering clouds had released their burden and it had begun to snow fairly heavily.

Sarah glanced around in the darkness and could see no one stirring. The only sounds were the hissing of the fire as snow fell into it, and the occasional snorting and snoring of the sleeping cowboys all around them.

She reached over and nudged Smoke with her hand, holding her finger to her lips when he came instantly awake and stared at her face in the meager light of the coals.

Without saying a word, she slipped a clasp knife into his hand. When he raised his eyebrows in question, she pointed toward the nearby mountains, even though they were not visible through the storm.

Smoke nodded and eased the knife open. It took him less than five seconds to saw through the ropes on his wrists and scramble to his feet.

He looked toward the line of horses tied to a rope stretched between two trees, but Sarah saw his glance and shook her head.

He shrugged, smiled, and grabbed up his blanket from the ground. Throwing it over his shoulders, he waved to her, and seconds later he had disappeared into the billowing white clouds of the snowstorm.

Sarah took another look around to make sure no one had seen what she'd done, and then she crawled back to her blankets, mussing the snow behind her to hide her tracks.

On the other side of the fire, Cletus shook his head and smiled at her actions. He had never been more proud of her in all the years he'd known her.

Sighing, he lay his head back down on his saddle and pulled the blanket up to his chin. Maybe, with a little luck, Jensen could get to the mountains before daylight and their moral dilemma would be solved.

"Can't kill a man who ain't there," he mumbled to himself, and fell fast asleep.

Nineteen

Monte Carson, acknowledging Pearlie's superior tracking skills, let him lead the way up the trail northward toward Pueblo.

Pearlie leaned over the side of his mount, and sometimes he even dismounted to squat next to some tracks, as he looked for the telltale signs of the passage of a wagon with new iron rims on the wheels. This caused the group to move slowly, something Cal in his youthfulness chaffed at.

"Jiminy, Pearlie, can't you go no faster'n that?" he complained.

Louis glanced over at him. "It won't do much good to race along, making good time, if we're going in the wrong direction, Cal." Louis looked up at the sky. "And this snow covering up the tracks isn't helping matters any either."

"I know, I know," Cal agreed. "It's just that I'm really worried about Smoke."

Sally smiled grimly. "We all are, Cal, but we mustn't let that keep us from doing the right thing in searching for him. It is very difficult to keep a clear mind when one is worried or frightened, but that is precisely when it is most important to do so."

Suddenly, up ahead, Pearlie got down off his horse and knelt next to some tracks just to the side of the road. "Looky, here," he called, pointing down. "Here's where the wagon got off the road a little bit an' outta all the other tracks. It's our buckboard, all right," he said, swinging back up into the saddle.

Monte grinned, taking out his six-gun and opening the loading gate to check his loads. "Now, we can ride full out and see if we can catch up to those . . . owlhoots," he said, glancing at Sally and editing his last few words so as not to offend her.

"But not too fast, Monte," Louis advised. "We don't want to ride so fast we run up on the scoundrels without being ready for them, something easy to do in a storm like this. That could get Smoke killed in a hurry."

Monte nodded and set his hat down tight on his head. He leaned over the saddle horn, spurred his horse, and kicked it into a gallop, with the others following right behind with bandannas tied over their noses and faces to help against the frigid north wind they were riding right into.

★ ★ ★

Meanwhile, up ahead a few miles, Bob Bartlett, Juan Gomez, and Billy Free had taken up positions on either side of the trail where it narrowed between two large outcroppings of boulders. The forest on either side of the trail was very thick with brush and the land there had a steep slope to it, which would make it almost impossible for anyone to move around and flank them without becoming targets from the high ground.

"How're we gonna know who to stop, Bob?" Billy asked. "How're we gonna be able to tell if they're trackin' Jensen or not, especially in this storm? Hell, I can't see shit through all this snow."

"Don't much matter, Billy," Bob answered. "For the next twelve hours or so, till it gets full on dark, we're gonna stop anybody an' everbody who tries to come up that there trail. That way we can be sure nobody can catch up to us 'fore we get to the ranch in Pueblo."

"But I don't hanker on killin' no innocent people, Bob," Billy said, his forehead creased in a frown. "I know Jensen deserves what he's gonna get, but shooting down some regular men who just happen to be in a posse just don't seem right to me," he complained.

"I didn't say nothin' 'bout killin' nobody, Billy," Bob said. He looked around at the spot they had chosen to defend the trail. "From up here, we can keep anybody from passin' without having to kill 'em. We just shoot a couple of hosses out from under the riders, hit some rocks close by 'em, an' I have a feelin' they gonna be hightailin' it back to Big Rock." He paused and added, "An' the way this snow is fallin', they'll play hell getting a clear shot back at us."

Billy nodded, relieved. He glanced across the trail to where Juan Gomez was sitting looking over a large rock. "You think Gomez got that message too?" he asked. "Ol' Juan likes to use his gun a little too much for my taste."

Bob followed his glance. "He'd better of gotten the message, since I told him flat out if he killed anybody Angus would have his scalp. The old man don't want this to turn into a range war. He just wants his revenge on the man that killed his son."

Suddenly, from across the trail came a low whistle. When they looked, they saw Juan pointing down at the trail as it rose to meet them.

A couple of hundred yards away, five riders could barely be seen riding at speed up the road into the teeth of the storm. Bob held up his hand to keep Juan from firing too soon, and he and Billy lay down across the top of the rock they were behind and took careful aim with their Winchesters.

Once the riders got in range, Bob gently squeezed the trigger on his long gun.

Down below, the rider in the lead was thrown head over heels as his horse swallowed its head and collapsed underneath him.

As the other riders jerked their mounts to a halt, both Billy and Juan fired at the same time. Billy missed, but the horse Juan was aiming at screamed and crow-hopped for a few seconds before it too fell to the ground.

Louis struggled to get his leg out from under his big Morgan. When the horse fell, it trapped Louis's leg underneath it.

Sally jumped off the big Palouse she was riding and ran to Monte's side. She gently rolled him over and found he was conscious, but barely. The unexpected fall had clearly stunned him badly.

She looked around quickly. There was no good cover nearby. They'd have to retreat at least a hundred yards back up the trail to find someplace to hide.

Pearlie jumped down off his horse and ran to help her, while Cal did the same with Louis. In minutes, supporting him between them, Sally and Pearlie were moving Monte back up the trail and away from the ambushers.

Louis, once Cal had helped him get up, took a moment to put a bullet into the head of his wounded horse so he wouldn't suffer. One look at Monte's mount told him the gelding was already dead, so Louis swung up into the saddle behind Cal and they galloped back up the trail heading for cover.

When they came abreast of Sally and Pearlie, who were still struggling with a dazed and incoherent Monte, Louis swung out of the saddle and took Sally's place helping Pearlie, while Sally rushed to get control of hers and Pearlie's horses and keep them with them.

As they hustled Monte up the trail, Louis looked back over his shoulder toward the place where the shots had come from. The snow was blowing so hard he could barely see the spot, and he was surprised there hadn't been any more gunplay. He knew the men hiding up there could have killed them had they so desired, even with the reduced visibility of the snowstorm. Why they hadn't was a mystery he didn't have time to puzzle out now. He had to get Monte under cover and then determine if he needed immediate medical help.

Up on the ridge, Bob nodded in satisfaction. They'd done a good job stopping those pilgrims from getting up the trail. He had no idea who they were, whether they were a posse after Jensen or not, but it didn't make any difference. No one was going to pass their way on this day, no matter who they were.

"You see that, Bob?" Billy asked.

"What?"

"I think one of those people was a woman," he answered. "I could see her long, black hair hanging out from under her hat when she ran to that man that was on the ground."

"So?" Bob asked.

"I just can't believe if'n that was a posse that they'd let a woman ride along. Leastways, I ain't never seen no woman on a posse before."

"Like I said before," Bob said, "it don't matter none who's down there. The fact is, it's our job to keep everybody from passing."

He looked back over his shoulder. "Now, I'll keep an eye on those galoots down there, an' you can get back there an' stir up that fire. I'm thinkin' some hot coffee'd sure go down good right now to take the chill out of my bones."

Down below, Sally had laid Monte down on his back and was sponging his forehead with cool water from her canteen. As snowflakes began to accumulate on his shirt, she had Pearlie cover him with a blanket.

"How are you feeling, Monte?" she asked when he began to shiver.

"I . . . I don't rightly know, Sally," he said with a confused look in his eyes. "Where are we and what happened to me?" he asked with a groan.

"We're on the trail after Smoke's kidnappers, Monte, and someone shot your horse out from under you, causing you to take a bad fall."

"Smoke's kidnappers?" he asked, clearly still confused and unsure of what was going on.

Louis frowned and touched Sally on the shoulder, indicating he wanted to talk with her out of Monte's hearing.

She got up and they walked a short distance away, turning their backs to the north wind to lessen the chill. "I think he's got a concussion, Sally," he said. "I've seen it before when someone got hit on the head. It makes them forget what they've done the past few days, and it can be very serious."

"I know," she said, glancing back over her shoulder at Monte's pale face. "We've got to get him back to Big Rock where Dr. Spalding can take a look at him."

"You think he's fit to ride a horse?" Louis asked, doubt in his voice.

"Not by himself," she answered. "But if you ride behind him and help hold him in the saddle, I think he can do it." She glanced up at the snowflakes drifting down. "He's going to have to, Louis. This storm looks like it's going to be pretty bad, and I don't know if he will survive a night of freezing temperatures, not in his condition."

"I agree," Louis said. He looked around at the terrain surrounding them. "Anyway, they've got us pretty well boxed in here, and I don't see any way past them without a larger force of men." He grinned sourly. "And especially not with the five of us having only three horses left."

Sally went back over to Monte. "Monte, we're going to try and get you up on a horse," she said. "Louis is going to ride with you on the way back to Big Rock."

As Pearlie and Cal helped Monte to his feet, he leaned over and vomited in the weeds. Louis glanced at Sally and shook his head. He knew from past experience this was not a good sign in men with head injuries.

It took both Cal and Pearlie to get Monte up on the horse and to hold him there while Louis climbed up behind him. "You just hold on to the saddle horn, Monte, and I'll do the riding for both of us," Louis said, putting his arms around Monte to grab the reins.

Since she was the lightest, Sally rode double with Cal while Pearlie had his own horse to himself.

"Pearlie, since you're riding alone, why don't you hightail it on back to Big Rock and see if you can get the doc to come out to meet us with a buckboard? That way he can get to see Monte sooner," Louis suggested.

Pearlie touched his hat and put the spurs to his mount, heading back down the trail as fast as he could ride.

It was slow going as they rode toward home. Louis was afraid to push the horse too fast lest he stumble in the snow or jar

Monte and cause more problems inside his head.

"Who do you think that was back there that shot us up?" Cal asked as they rode.

"It must have been some of the people that took Smoke," Sally said.

"I wonder why they didn't try and kill us," Louis said. "They certainly had a good chance to do so."

Sally shook her head. "I don't know, Louis. Perhaps their only quarrel is with Smoke and they don't want to kill anyone else unless they have to."

"But if they're that angry with Smoke, why take him?" Louis asked. "Once they had the drop on him, why didn't they just kill him and be done with it? That would have been a lot less dangerous and would have made a lot more sense than taking him prisoner."

"I don't know, Louis," Sally said, "but I do intend to find out, and God help whoever is behind this."

Louis glanced at Sally and felt the hairs on the back of his neck stir. He'd seen that look before in Smoke's eyes, and it always meant someone was about to die.

Suddenly, he felt very sorry for whoever had taken Smoke, for he knew their days were numbered.

Twenty

Smoke moved through the night as fast as he could, considering the snowstorm made the darkness almost absolute and he was running through snow that was getting deeper by the minute. It was only his excellent night vision that kept him from breaking an ankle or impaling himself on a tree limb or other natural obstruction in the heavy forest he was traversing.

Knowing the storm, like most early fall storms, was coming almost directly out of the north, he realized all he had to do to keep on track was to keep the wind directly in his face. That way he avoided traveling in circles as most inexperienced men did when moving in unfamiliar territory.

Smoke knew the mountain ranges all around them were closest directly to the north, and getting up into the High Lonesome was his only chance to avoid the men who would surely be on his trail no later than daybreak.

He knew from earlier in the day that the closest mountain was about seven miles away and that he had absolutely no chance to make it before daylight, not on foot traveling through darkness in snow that was rapidly getting up to his mid-calves. The only good thing about his rapid advance was that the exertion was keeping his body temperature high enough to avoid frostbite due to exposure to the extreme cold.

The bad news was that his only weapon was a five-inch clasp knife and he was completely without any other supplies or food. He laughed out loud into the freezing north wind. Only a mountain man, and a crazy one at that, would think that he had any chance at all against more than a dozen well-armed men on horseback on his trail under these conditions.

Well, this crazy old mountain man still had a few tricks up his sleeve, and if he could keep from freezing to death long enough, he'd show them a thing or two.

The wind was howling and the snow was blowing almost horizontally when the camp began to wake up the next morning. Dawn was evident only through a general lightening up of the snow since there was no morning sun to be seen.

Cletus, as usual, was the first to arise,

and he piled fresh wood onto the smoldering coals of last night's campfire. He filled pots with water and heaping handfuls of coffee in preparation for an early breakfast. He knew from his observation the night before that Smoke Jensen had escaped his bonds, but he pretended not to notice the empty space where Smoke had lain the previous night as he busied himself around the fire.

As men slowly gathered around the fire, holding out hands to get them warm and gratefully accepting mugs of steaming coffee, he told Jimmy Corbett to get started cooking some fatback and beans in the large skillets they'd brought along.

"Don't worry with trying to make biscuits in this storm," he said. "We've still got some left from last night's dinner that ought'a do."

"Gonna have to dip them sinkers in coffee to get 'em soft enough to chew," Jason Biggs said, grinning. "Otherwise you're liable to break a tooth on 'em."

Cletus was about to reply when Wally Stevens hollered from over near the tree Smoke had been under, "Hey, ever'body, Jensen's gone!"

Cletus forced a surprised look on his face and ran over to where Smoke was supposed to be lying. "Well, I'll be damned," he exclaimed, straightening up and looking around with his hands on his hips. "The bastard's not here."

"I don't see no ropes," Stevens said, looking around on the ground and pushing mounds of snow aside, "so maybe he couldn't get them loose and his hands are still tied."

"What's going on here?" Sarah asked as she appeared out of the blowing snow.

"Looks like Jensen has somehow managed to escape from the camp," Cletus said, trying to appear disgusted with the turn of events.

"Escaped?" Sarah asked, her voice astounded. "How in the world was he able to do that?"

"I don't know, Miss MacDougal," Biggs said, "but he can't have gotten far in this storm, not on foot."

"How do you know he didn't take one of the horses?" she asked, causing everyone to make a mad dash off to the side where the horses were all tied to a tether rope.

After a quick count, Cletus assured everyone that Smoke hadn't in fact taken any of the mounts.

The men went back to the camp and began to make a circle around the periphery, trying to locate any tracks Smoke might have left.

After an hour of searching, they all decided the storm had covered any traces he might have made.

They gathered around the fire to get warm again and to discuss what they ought to do. "You got any bright ideas, Clete?" Biggs asked. " 'Cause I surely don't relish going back to the ranch and having Mr. MacDougal chew my ears off for letting Jensen get away from us."

Cletus thought for a moment as he finished off his mug of coffee. Finally, he looked around. "All right, here is what I think. Jensen could have gone in only two directions, north or south."

"Why do you say that?" Stevens asked.

" 'Cause if he headed either east or west, all he's gonna find is a big prairie with almost no cover to speak of. Jensen's too smart to put himself in that position, 'cause in this weather, no cover means he'd freeze to death. Now, if he heads south back towards his home, we got three men behind us guarding the trail. If, on the other hand, he heads north towards the nearest mountain range, then he's got a good chance of hiding out from us if he makes it."

"So," Sarah said, "you think he's probably gone north toward the mountains?"

Cletus shrugged. "It's what I'd do in his place." He made a grimace of disgust. " 'Course, we're gonna have to cover all the directions, just in case he tried to fool us by going someplace we wouldn't think he'd try."

"That's gonna split us up pretty good," Stevens said.

"Not really," Sarah said. "Remember, Jensen's on foot and doesn't have any weapons. We can send one man east and one man west. If he's out there in the open, they should be able to run him down before nightfall and take him prisoner again."

"What about south?" Cletus asked.

"I think one man should be able to get back down the trail and warn Bartlett and Gomez and Free to be on the lookout for him," she said. "That should leave us plenty of men to undertake a campaign to catch him before he can get too far into the mountains if he headed north."

Cletus shook his head in admiration. "Missy, I wish I'd had you running my outfit during the war. You plumb got a mind for tactics."

"Well, I'd suggest we get a move on," she said. "Clete, you pick the men to go east and west and south, and I'll see to getting their canteens filled with hot coffee to keep them from freezing to death on the way."

"We got time to eat first, Miss MacDougal?" Stevens asked, his face hopeful.

"Certainly. We can't go out into this storm on a manhunt with our bellies empty, now can we, men?"

Cletus laughed. "Jimmy, get those beans to cookin', boy, we got a man to catch."

"Yes, sir," Corbett answered, using a long stick to stir the coals under the trestle that contained the pot of beans and fatback.

As Sarah began to fill canteens with hot coffee, Cletus looked at her and shook his head. He'd never seen a better performance. No one would ever suspect that she'd let Jensen go herself, and he damn sure wasn't going to enlighten anyone.

He stepped over to the edge of the fire and stood looking into the north wind, in the direction Jensen must have gone if he was to have any chance to avoid capture.

What would it take for a man to have the courage to take off on foot into a blizzard like this with no weapons and no warm clothes to speak of? he wondered.

He chuckled to himself, knowing full

well the answer to that question. A man would have to be completely without hope of survival otherwise to take a chance like that, and Jensen certainly knew that for him to stay in camp would mean certain death.

As Sarah called to him that the beans and fatback were ready, he turned and shook his head. The man didn't stand a chance in this weather, he thought, but at least freezing to death was probably less painful than a bullet.

Twenty-one

Pearlie jerked his horse to a stop in front of Dr. Colton Spalding's office, bounded out of the saddle, and raced through the front door without bothering to knock.

Spalding, who was called Cotton by all of his friends due to his ash-blond, almost white hair, looked up from his rolltop desk in the corner of his parlor. When he saw the agitation in Pearlie's face, he got to his feet and began putting on his coat before the young man had a chance to speak.

"Doc, you gotta come!" Pearlie gasped, still out of breath from his breakneck ride into town.

Cotton picked up his black bag and a pair of gloves from the side table in the hallway. "Of course, Pearlie," he said. "Is there trouble out at the Sugarloaf?"

"No, Doc, it's Monte Carson," Pearlie answered. "His hoss was shot out from under him and he took a terrible fall. He hit his head an' he ain't been exactly actin' right since then."

"Where is he?" Cotton asked as they exited his door, followed by his wife Mona, who'd heard the commotion and joined them in the parlor. He gave Mona a quick kiss good-bye and told her he'd be back as soon as possible. When she went back in the door, he didn't bother to lock it in case someone needing his care wanted to come in and wait for his return, in which case his wife Mona, who was also his nurse, would take care of that person.

"Out on the road north of town, 'bout five or six miles by now," he answered.

"By now?" Cotton asked, raising his eyebrows. "Don't tell me he is being moved."

"Uh . . . yes, sir," Pearlie said. "Louis is riding double with him to keep him on horseback."

"Oh, sweet Jesus," Cotton said under his breath as he climbed up into his wagon that was hitched in front of his office.

"You'd better take me there as fast as you can, Pearlie, and let us hope we're not too late and that moving him has not caused irreparable damage to his brain."

When they met up with Louis and Sally and Cal on the road into town, Cotton pulled his wagon to the side of the road. "Pearlie, scrape that snow out of the back of the wagon and get those blankets out from under the tarp there under the seat. Make a bed for Monte as best you can."

Monte was sitting unconscious in front of Louis, being held in place by Louis's hands around him. The sheriff's head lolled limply to and fro as the horse moved.

"Cal, get over here and help me take Monte down and get him in the back of my wagon, but be as gentle as you can," the doctor ordered.

Moments later, Monte was lying on his back in the rear compartment of Cotton's wagon and the doctor was leaning over him, checking his pupils and feeling of his pulse.

"Has he had any violent purging . . . uh, vomiting?" he asked Sally.

"Yes, once, right after he tried to get up after the fall," she answered.

Cotton shook his head. "That's not a good sign. It means he's definitely had a concussion."

Sally, standing at his side, said, "I know a head injury shouldn't be moved, Cotton, but I thought the time saved getting him under your care and out of the cold was worth the danger of moving him." She gave Monte a worried look. "There was no shelter on the trail and we had no way of keeping him warm in this storm."

"You're probably right, Sally," Cotton said, not looking away from his patient. "At any rate, it's hard to say which is worse, exposure to the elements or movement."

He straightened up after tucking the blankets around Monte to keep him as warm as possible. "Now, I need to get him back to my office where he can be properly cared for."

As he climbed up onto the seat of the wagon, he looked back down at Sally. "Perhaps you'd better swing back by Monte's house and tell Mary what is going on," he said. "She can come to my office and sit with him if she wishes."

"How serious is it, Cotton?" Sally asked.

The doctor shrugged. "Well, it's a good sign that he survived the trip on horseback. He's obviously had some minor bleeding in his head and a severe concussion. The only question now is will he have any more and just how much damage what he's already had has done to his mind." As he took up the reins, he added, "He's going to need some luck."

After Cotton slapped the reins on his horses' rears and moved off down the trail, Louis asked Sally, "What do we do about Smoke?"

She shook her head. "First, I need to go talk to Mary and tell her what happened." She hesitated. "We can't do Smoke any good right now, not with those men blocking the trail."

"Miss Sally," Cal said, "we could get a big posse together in less time than it takes to say it. Heck, just about ever'body in Big Rock would go along if'n they thought Smoke was in trouble."

"He's correct, Sally," Louis agreed. "With a large number of men we could get by that ambush and go after the men who took Smoke."

Sally turned tortured eyes to Louis. "Yes, Louis, I believe we could do that. But how many men would get hurt or possibly killed trying to get past that ambush site?"

When he paused, unable to answer, Sally smiled sadly. "See what I mean? Do you think Smoke would want a lot of towns-people getting hurt trying to rescue him?"

Louis reluctantly shook his head. "No, I guess not, Sally."

She put a hand on his shoulder. "Look at it this way. If whoever took him wanted to kill him, he's already dead. If he's still alive by now, then there is some other reason for taking him and keeping him alive. Either way, waiting until morning to continue our trip after them won't make much difference."

"You think the men guarding the trail will be gone by then?" Pearlie asked.

She nodded. "Probably. They cannot hope to hold the trail forever. My guess is they were just trying to give whoever has Smoke time to get to where they're going. We should be able to get by in the morning."

"I just hope we're not too late for Smoke," Cal said, his voice heavy.

Sally swung up into the saddle and smiled. "Cal, you should have more faith in Smoke. He has managed to survive much worse than this for a lot of years."

Louis laughed as he kicked his horse to follow Sally. "That's a fact!" he said.

Just as Cletus and Sarah and their men were saddling up their mounts, Daniel Macklin approached Cletus. "Say, Clete, I think somebody ought'a ride on over to the ranch and tell Angus what's goin' on," he said, his eyes flicking from Sarah to Cletus, not sure who was in charge of the men since she'd arrived.

Cletus tightened the cinch-belt on his saddle and said over his shoulder, "And just why would you think that, Mac, since

Angus put me in charge of this little fracas?"

Macklin rubbed his jaw. "Well, for starters, you got four men coverin' our back trail, an' two more headin' off east and west, so that only leaves six or seven of us to head out after Jensen in the mountains."

"So, I say again, Mac, what is your point?"

"I done some talkin' 'bout Jensen when I was in his town waiting for Sarah to make up her mind what to do," Macklin said, glancing at her out of the corner of his eye to make sure she wasn't taking his talk wrong.

"Yeah, so?"

"What I found out was this Jensen is not only a famous gunfighter, he was a mountain man from the time he was a little boy until just a few years ago."

Now Macklin had Cletus's full attention. "Is that a fact?" Cletus said, his lips tight.

"Yep, an' you know that a handful of us cowboys ain't gonna be no match for a mountain man up in those mountains," Macklin said, glancing off in the direction of the snow-covered peaks to the north, barely visible in the light snowfall.

Cletus followed his gaze. "You may be

right, Mac. Of course, I'm hoping to catch up to Jensen 'fore he gets a chance to get up into those mountains."

Macklin shrugged. "If you do, then you'll be able to handle him with no problem, assuming you catch him out in the open." He hesitated. "Of course, if you don't, you're gonna need all the help you can get."

Cletus glanced at Sarah, who was busily cinching up her saddle and pretending not to be paying any attention to their talk. Cletus was caught in a dilemma. He wanted Jensen to do exactly what Macklin said he was worried about, that is, get up into the mountains and disappear so they couldn't find him and take him back to Angus. But he didn't want Angus to suspect as much, so he had to play the game of doing his best to capture the gunman.

"I guess you're right, Mac. Why don't you hightail it on ahead to the ranch and see if Angus wants to hire more men to come out here and help us hunt Jensen down if he makes it to the mountains? That way, we can leave it up to Angus how much he really wants Jensen."

Macklin nodded. "My thoughts exactly, Clete."

Cletus thought for a moment, and then

he added, "If you do bring more men, plan to meet up with us at that old line cabin at the base of the mountain near where that stream comes out onto flat ground."

Mac nodded and he swung up into his saddle, tipped his hat, and put the spurs to his mount, heading up the road toward the MacDougal ranch in Pueblo.

Cletus looked over at Sarah to see how she was taking this, but all he could see was that her jaw was set and her lips were tightly squeezed together as she finished setting her saddle and throwing her saddlebags across the animal's rump.

"That all right with you, Sarah?" he asked.

She turned to look at him, still not realizing he knew she'd been the one to turn Smoke loose. "Sure, Clete. What Mac said made sense, and we may well need some help if Jensen makes it up into those slopes."

Cletus put his foot in his stirrup and eased up onto the back of his horse. "I just hope Angus don't send a bunch of flatlanders that don't know which end of a gun the bullet comes out of to help us. Otherwise, we're gonna need more'n one wagon to carry all the bodies back in."

Twenty-two

Instead of trying to run the entire several miles to the lower slopes of the nearest mountain and exhausting himself, Smoke alternated walking at a fast pace with jogging for fifty yards. He kept his head lowered and his eyes squinted against the blowing snow and wind in his face, but even so, it wasn't long before his eyes began to burn and itch from the drying effects of the constant wind.

He'd known men up in the mountains who'd had their eyes frozen shut by blizzards like this, and he didn't want to take any chances, so he kept the brim of his hat down low and his head bent down, glancing up occasionally to make sure he wasn't about to walk into a crevice or boulder.

Soon, the snow had accumulated to a depth almost up to his knees, and it was beginning to make walking extremely difficult and running impossible. He knew he was going to have trouble getting to deep cover on the mountainside before dawn. The only good thing about the amount of snow falling was that it would completely obliterate his tracks so if the gang of men tried to follow them, they wouldn't be able to find him, and it would slow them down as much as it was him.

Normally, faced with a storm such as this and no horse, Smoke would cut some branches off pine trees and build himself a lean-to to weather out the storm out of the wind. With ten or so angry men on his trail, this wasn't an option, but if he didn't do something to get out of the weather, he was going to freeze to death while he walked. His only hope was to make it until dawn lightened the eastern sky so he could find something else that would do to both hide him and keep him out of the cold.

By the time the eastern sky began to lighten enough for him to see his surroundings, Smoke was shivering with cold and was weak from dehydration. His sweat had frozen on his skin and his mouth was so dry he couldn't work up a good spit.

He resisted the urge to eat snow, as that would only lower his body temperature. He knew of several mountain men who'd made that mistake and hadn't lived to tell about it.

As the day got brighter, Smoke noticed a fallen ponderosa pine off to his right. It appeared to have been struck by lightning, as there was a jagged, blackened scar along its trunk.

He slogged over to it, and saw to his relief that the giant had taken out several other smaller trees around it when it crashed to the ground. Smoke moved along the trunk until he came to the jumble of broken and crushed limbs at the top of the tree. Sure enough, it was as he'd hoped. The tangle of tree limbs and trunks and roots made a perfectly acceptable place to get out of sight and weather out the rest of the storm.

With any luck, the men chasing him would just ride on by if they came this way.

Smoke pushed aside a thick branch and bent over to worm his way into the thick tangle. He froze when he heard a low growl from in front of him. He realized immediately what it was. It was the sound of a mountain cougar who'd had the same idea of using the tree for shelter as Smoke had.

Moving slowly, Smoke took out the small clasp knife and worked the blade open, trying not to provoke the big cat into a charge. He couldn't see the animal in the gloom of the enclosure, but he could smell its fetid breath and musky odor as if it was very close.

Suddenly the cat snarled and rushed at him out of the darkness of the jumble of tree limbs. Smoke jumped back and let go of the branch he'd been bending back to enter. The branch snapped forward, catching the cougar in the face as it leapt at Smoke.

Smoke dove onto the cat before it could regain its balance and slashed to and fro with the small knife, praying he'd hit the throat before the cat got his arm in its powerful jaws.

They rolled over a couple of times, Smoke almost screaming at the burning pain as the cat raked his back with its claws. Luckily, the intervening branch kept the cougar from gutting Smoke with its hind feet as cougars usually did.

Moments later, it was over. The cougar gasped its last breath as Smoke's knife tore its throat open almost to the spine.

Unable to see the damage to his back, Smoke did the next best thing. He pulled his shirt up and lay on his back in the snow, rocking back and forth and letting the coldness stop the bleeding and wash out his wounds.

The pain was almost unbearable, but he counted himself lucky to be alive and a little pain was a small price to pay for shelter, and now food. He sat up and pulled his shirt back down over his back, wincing as the deerskin scraped the raw wounds. He had no way of knowing if the bleeding had stopped, but figured he'd find out soon enough if the blood soaked the shirt.

He didn't dare start a fire, so he quickly skinned the cougar and gutted it. Since liver has the most nutrients, Smoke ate as much of the raw liver as his stomach could take. Once he'd filled his belly, he scraped the skin as best he could and cut it into wide pieces he could wrap around his lower legs as leggings, to keep from getting frostbite when he walked through deep snow. It wouldn't smell very good, he thought with a smile, but that was the least of his worries.

With the still-warm liver in his stomach, he risked eating enough snow to slake his thirst, and then he curled up in the crown of the fallen tree under a blanket of pine boughs and the rest of the cougar skin. He was asleep instantly.

Cletus took the lead, with Sarah right behind him, as the group headed through the forest toward the mountain whose peak couldn't be seen through the driving snow.

Even though they were on horseback, they couldn't move much faster than Smoke had been able to because of the depth of the snow and the uneven, wooded terrain.

"Hey, Boss," George Jones called from the middle of the pack.

"Yeah, George?" Cletus answered, twisting in his saddle to see what the man wanted.

"Maybe it'd be a good idea if we spread out 'stead of riding in a line like this. In this storm, it's better'n even odds Jensen froze to death last night. It'd be a shame to ride past his carcass and not know it."

Cletus had to admit the man had a good point. Though he didn't for a minute think a mountain man would ever freeze to death in a minor storm like this, Cletus knew that Jensen might well have gone to ground somewhere between here and the mountain hoping they'd ride right on past him.

"That's a good idea, George," Cletus said, stopping his horse. He waved his hands to both sides. "I want you men to spread out, and keep a sharp eye for any sign of Jensen along the way," he called. "And be sure to stay in sight of the men on either side of you. I don't want Jensen to be able to slip between us."

In a lower voice, he said, "Sarah, I want you to stay next to me. Your daddy'd have my hide if I let anything happen to you."

Sarah gave him a gentle smile. They both knew she could shoot every bit as straight as him and she was probably a lot faster on the draw. Still and all, he'd been a good and loyal friend to both her and her father, so she didn't point this out to him. "All right, Clete. I'll stay close so you can protect me from the big, bad Smoke Jensen."

He frowned at her, knowing she was putting him on. "Don't underestimate this man, Sarah. I know you don't think he is a really bad man, but men who are desperate to live will sometimes do things they wouldn't ordinarily do — and that includes Smoke Jensen."

Sarah had a hard time imagining Smoke Jensen would ever be desperate, but she kept her mouth shut and rode alongside Cletus as he moved northward toward the nearest mountain. She pulled her heavy, fur-lined deerskin coat tight around her shoulders as they rode into the freezing wind, wondering how Jensen, who was dressed only in buckskins, would be able to survive the brutal conditions.

★ ★ ★

Even though they were downwind, Smoke heard the approaching riders when they were still over a hundred yards away, and he came instantly awake. Years living in the High Lonesome had trained him to be able to hear and see things most normal men couldn't, and he could respond to them instinctively without having to think about it beforehand.

It was a trait that'd saved his life on more than one occasion when he and Preacher were living up in the High Lonesome.

He eased to the edge of his tree-limb hideout and glanced around to make sure the snow had covered all signs of the struggle with the big cat. He nodded in satisfaction to see a pristine blanket of fresh snow around the jumble of fallen trees he was in. He was also relieved to see that the storm was still fairly heavy. He was counting on it to mask his next moves.

He readied himself by moving to the very edge of his hideout so that he could exit it quickly and silently when the time came, and then he got out the clasp knife and opened it. He was going to need it very soon now.

Trying to keep a straight line of riders

going into a storm and weaving back and forth in a fairly thick forest is impossible. Thus, the line of riders coursing through the woods toward Smoke was ragged and uneven, with some men being fifty or sixty yards ahead of or behind the others on either side of them. The fury of the storm kept conversation between the riders at a minimum, and most were riding with their heads down and their hats pulled low over their brows to try to keep the worst of the wind and snow out of their faces.

Smoke knew he could just lie still, and odds were that the men would pass him by and he'd be safe for a while. But he'd still be without a horse, and this put him at a terrible disadvantage in the deadly game of hide and seek they were playing. No, he couldn't afford to let them go by. He needed both weapons and a horse if he was going to survive this death hunt.

He hated the idea of killing a man he didn't even know, but the man must've known what he was doing when he signed on to take another man to his certain death. Smoke knew it was much too dangerous with the other men so close to try to take a man's guns and horse and leave him alive, so he steeled himself to the inevitable; he was going to have to hit fast and

hard and not worry about the conse-
quences.

Smoke waited until a figure on horseback was directly opposite his hiding place.
As the man moved just past him, Smoke
eased out of the tree limbs and took a running jump up on the back of the man's
horse. As he landed, he wrapped his left
arm around the man's face and, with the
knife in his right hand, he made a rapid
slashing motion across the man's throat.

The horse reared up and whinnied, but
the sound was lost in the howling of the
wind.

Smoke held on tight as the man's body
struggled for a few seconds and then became limp as his hot blood spurted across
Smoke's forearm.

When he was completely limp, Smoke
eased the man's hat off and put it firmly on
his own head, throwing his own hat to the
ground. Next, he took the man's gun belt
and holster and put it around his waist.
The hardest part was removing the man's
thick rawhide and fur coat without letting
his body fall off the horse, which Smoke
kept moving by gentle nudges of his heels,
guiding the animal with his knees.

When he had the man's hat, guns, and
coat on, Smoke started to let the body fall,

and then thought better of it. Leaning to the side, he felt in the man's right boot. Sure enough, there was a long-bladed skinning knife there. It would be of much more use to Smoke than the small clasp knife he'd used to kill the man.

Looking to both sides to make sure he'd been unobserved so far, Smoke waited until a particularly strong flurry of snow came, and then let the man's body fall to the side, where it landed in a snowbank with a soft thud inaudible from more than a few feet away.

Slowly, so as not to draw too much attention to himself, Smoke let the horse he was riding ease on out ahead of the line of men. Before long, the men on either side of him were barely visible in the blowing snow. Smoke knew the storm couldn't last too much longer, and he planned to be well away before the snow stopped and he became fully visible to the others. He hoped with the limited visibility of the storm, the man's hat and coat would fool his friends into thinking Smoke was him.

Suddenly, a voice called from about forty yards behind him. "Hey, Charlie, what's your hurry?"

Smoke hunched over, tightening his grip on the reins. He knew he didn't have much longer before his ruse was discovered.

"Yeah, Blake," another voice on the other side hollered. "Get your ass back here with the rest of us 'fore we accidentally put a bullet in your butt thinkin' you're Jensen."

As he passed a tight grove of trees, Smoke leaned forward and dug his heels into his mount, causing it to break into a full gallop ahead.

"Hey, what the . . . ?" a voice yelled.

And then, another screamed, "Yo, Clete! Somethin's wrong with Charlie Blake. He's ridin' like a bat outta hell!"

The man on Smoke's right kicked his horse into a gallop also, wanting to see why his friend was racing ahead. As he pulled closer, he realized it wasn't Charlie Blake on the horse ahead of him.

"Damn! That ain't Charlie, fellers, that's Jensen," he screamed, pulling his pistol out and opening fire.

He might have caught Smoke, but a branch suddenly appeared in front of him and whipped across his face, drawing blood and making him slow his horse to keep from falling off.

The ghostly figure on horseback in front of him disappeared into the gloomy snow-storm ahead.

Cletus and Sarah rode over to Sam

Jackson. "You all right, Sam?" Cletus asked.

Jackson sleeved blood off his face where the tree limb had slashed his cheek. "Yeah, I'll be all right," he growled, leaning over to spit blood from his mouth.

"You say that wasn't Charlie up there?" Sarah asked, looking ahead into the snow flurries.

"Naw, I don't think so," Jackson said. "He had Charlie's coat on, but he didn't sit a horse like Charlie an' he looked to be about thirty pounds heavier and five or six inches taller."

"But how did he get Charlie's coat and horse?" Cletus asked.

Jackson looked back over his shoulder. "I don't know, Boss, but I'll bet we ain't gonna find out what happened from Charlie either."

Cletus nodded. "All right, men, let's double back a ways and see if we can find Charlie's body."

Sarah took a deep breath and felt a deep sorrow. She didn't know Charlie Blake well, but if he was dead, then it was her fault for letting Smoke Jensen escape.

She shook her head as she pulled her horse's head around. How was she going to live with herself if more men were killed because of her? she wondered.

Twenty-three

As he rode hell-bent-for-leather through the deepening snow and into the teeth of the freezing north wind after capturing the man's horse, Smoke leaned as close to his mount's head as he could to avoid being scraped out of the saddle by a tree limb. He had to trust the horse's instinct not to run headlong into a tree or off a cliff, and so all he could do for the first couple of hundred yards of their flight was to hang on for dear life and hope for the best.

At least it beat a bullet in the back.

After about ten minutes at a full gallop, Smoke raised his head and looked back over his shoulder. The snow was still blowing, and all he could see was a solid sheet of white behind him.

He slowed the horse and cocked his head to the side, listening to see if he could hear any pursuit over the howling of the wind.

Nothing. He turned back around, pulled his hat down tight, and rode on into the wind toward the mountain up ahead, moving slower now to give his horse a rest. He knew that if he could make the slopes up ahead before his captors caught up to him, he would have the advantage for the first time since this adventure began.

He smiled grimly. And then it would be time to pay them back.

Angus MacDougal was just sitting down to a solitary supper, served by his house-keeper/cook, when the door banged open and a breathless Daniel Macklin barged in.

Angus threw down his napkin and smiled, evidently thinking the group of men had arrived with Smoke Jensen as their prisoner.

"Where is that son of a bitch?" Angus growled, moving toward the hat rack in the corner with his belt and holstered pistol hanging on it.

Macklin didn't understand at first what Angus was referring to. "Uh . . . where is who?" he asked, taking his hat off and holding it in front of him like a shield.

Angus sighed as he buckled on his gun belt. "Jensen, of course," he answered. "You remember him, don't you? The bastard who gunned my Johnny down? The man you went to Big Rock to get for me?"

"Uh . . . that's what I come to tell you, Mr. MacDougal." Few men in the world called Angus MacDougal by his first name, and certainly not an employee as low as Daniel Macklin.

Angus knew something was wrong. "Well, spit it out, man. What the hell's going on?"

"We were 'bout half a day's ride from here when Jensen somehow managed to get loose and run away," Macklin finally managed to say.

"What?" Angus yelled, advancing on Macklin as if he were about to kill him.

Macklin held up his hands. "Now wait a minute, Mr. MacDougal. He ain't gotten away — leastways not all the way away."

Angus slapped his thigh with his hand. "Now just what the hell does that mean?" he growled.

"He didn't get no horse, an' he's on foot in a bad storm some miles from the nearest mountain. He's runnin' on foot through the woods with Cletus and the rest of the men on horseback after him."

The redness began to fade a little bit from Angus's face at this news. "Oh, well, then, it shouldn't take Clete long to run him down then, should it?"

Macklin shook his head. "No, sir, I don't think so."

Suddenly Angus cocked an eyebrow at Macklin. "If that's so, then why did Clete send you here?"

"Well, the fact of the matter is that Jensen used to be a mountain man, sir, and we . . . that is, Cletus thought that if he did manage to make the mountains, we might ought'a have a few more men out looking for him."

Angus took a couple of long, slow breaths to try to calm himself. He found he did his best thinking when he was calm, not when he was in a fit of rage.

After a moment, he nodded. "I guess I can't argue with that logic," he said. "Let me see, you got about ten, eleven men up there now. Another ten or so ought'a be plenty. With twenty men I can run a search of the mountain that a squirrel couldn't get through."

He pulled out his pocket watch and opened the gold clasp. "Well, it's too late now to round up any good men. We'll get to bed early and be in Pueblo at dawn. We should be able to find ten men who want to make a little extra money without any problem."

Or who want to make the richest rancher for a hundred miles happy, Macklin thought.

"You have anything to eat 'fore you got on the way here?" he asked, suddenly in a better frame of mind now that he knew he'd have the personal pleasure of hunting Jensen down like the dog he was. Hell, it might even be fun running the bastard down like a deer or a bear.

"No, sir," Macklin answered, his mouth watering at the smell of the pot roast and fresh vegetables he could smell on the table in the next room.

Angus nodded. "Well, then, head on over to the bunkhouse and I'll have my cook send you over a plate."

"Thank you, sir," Macklin said, trying to hide his anger. Here he was busting his butt to help the old man out and he wasn't good enough to break bread with him in his house. The ungrateful asshole!

The next morning, just as the sun was peeking over the eastern slope mountains, Angus and Macklin were knocking on Sheriff Wally Tupper's door in Pueblo.

A sleepy Wally opened the door, his hair disarranged and his face creased with wrinkles from his pillow. "Yeah?" he asked gruffly before he saw who was on his doorstep.

Then it was, "Oh, I'm sorry, Mr.

MacDougal. Come on in and I'll have the wife fix you up some coffee and breakfast."

"Don't have time for that, Wally," Angus said, brushing past the sheriff into his house as if he owned it. "I need you to get dressed and help me round up ten or fifteen hard men to go on the trail with me."

"You mean, like a posse?" Wally asked, covering a wide yawn with the back of his hand.

"Kind'a," Angus replied enigmatically.

"Why . . . what for, Mr. MacDougal?" Wally asked as he pulled his trousers up under his nightshirt and sat on a couch to put on his socks.

"We're going polecat hunting," Angus said with an evil grin.

"What?" Wally asked again, pausing with one sock on and the other in his hand.

"My men were on the way back here with Smoke Jensen in tow, when he managed to get away. He's on foot and running for the mountains as we speak. I need some men to help me roust him out of those woods if Cletus doesn't find him first."

"But Mr. MacDougal, Jensen ain't broke no laws that I know of."

"So what?" Angus asked.

"Well, I can't hardly send no posse after

a man who ain't done nothing wrong."

Angus reached over, grabbed the front of Wally's nightshirt, and jerked his face close. "Wallace Tupper, if you don't want to spend the rest of your miserable life shooting stray dogs for fifty cents a piece in this town instead of being sheriff, you'd better make up your mind who you're gonna listen to . . . me or those god-damned law books you're always reading!"

"But Mr. MacDougal," Wally protested.

"But nothing, Wally," Angus growled. "Now I'm gonna go on over to the café on Main Street and have myself some coffee and maybe some eggs and bacon. If you aren't there with at least ten good men, by the time I finish, I'll assume you're out hunting for dogs to shoot."

Less than an hour later, while Angus was still sopping up egg yolks with a folded piece of pancake, Wally Tupper appeared at the café with twelve men. All of the men had a hard look about them and all were armed to the teeth.

Wally walked into the café, his hat in his hands. "Uh, I managed to get you twelve men, Mr. MacDougal," he said, not willing to meet Angus's eyes directly.

"That's a good man, Wally. I knew you'd

come through for me as usual."

"I told 'em since this wasn't an official posse, that you'd be paying them for the trip," Wally said, his voice low and uncertain, as if he were asking Angus instead of telling him how it was going to be.

Angus waved a hand. "No problem, Wally. Since this is personal, I really can't expect the town to pay for it, now can I?"

"Uh . . . no, sir. I guess not."

"Now, while I'm finishing up here, I want you to get a couple of packhorses and go on over to the general store and get a couple of crates of dynamite, some cans of black powder, lots of extra ammunition of various calibers, and enough grub for the men to be gone a week or so."

"Is there anything else?" Wally asked, struggling to keep his anger at being ordered around like he was one of Angus's employees out of his voice.

Angus shook his head. "No, I think that ought to do it for right now."

Wally put his hat on and walked from the café. As he walked toward the general store, he thought to himself, Crazy old coot! Serve his ass right if Jensen somehow manages to blow his fool head off. And just where does he get off ordering me around like I'm some ranch hand anyway?

By the time he got to the store, he was so mad he could hardly unclench his teeth to say hello to the proprietor when greeted.

He pointed behind the counter at the hundreds of boxes of ammunition. "Seymour, I'm gonna need a bunch of cartridges and other things, and I'm gonna need 'em fast."

Twenty-four

Sally sat on a wide settee in Dr. Spalding's parlor holding Mary Carson's hand. Mary was quietly sobbing into a lace handkerchief. Across the room, Pearlie and Cal sat in high-armed easy chairs, both of them acutely uncomfortable in the presence of a crying woman.

Finally, after what seemed like years but was only a couple of hours, Cotton Spalding emerged from his inner treatment room drying his hands on a towel. He looked dog-tired, with red, bloodshot eyes and dark circles under the eyes. He'd been continually by Monte's side during the long night, and it showed.

Mary looked up quickly, an unspoken question in her eyes. Cotton smiled at her and moved to take her hand. "He's going to be just fine, Mary. He's awake now and I can find no evidence of any brain damage or other infirmity, other than a complete amnesia about the events of the last couple of days, which isn't unusual in these cases."

"Oh, thank God!" Mary breathed, looking skyward.

Sally Jensen looked over at the boys, her eyes brimming with tears of thankfulness, while both Cal and Pearlie grinned from ear to ear.

"Now, he's going to have to remain quiet for a week or two, and I'm going to want you to feed him plenty of beef stew and soup with cream in it to get his strength back," Cotton said, his manner becoming more professional.

"Don't you worry, Doc Spalding," Mary said, nodding her head as she spoke. "I'll make sure that ornery galoot does exactly what you tell him to."

"It isn't going to be easy, Mary," Cotton said. "He's already chomping at the bit to get back to work. He asked me who was going to take care of his town if he lay around on his butt all day."

They all laughed at that. It was just like Monte Carson to put the welfare of the townspeople ahead of his own well-being. It was one reason why he'd never had any serious opposition for reelection as sheriff since Smoke had recommended him for the job when the town was first formed.

After the doctor went into another room to see to another patient, Mary turned to

Sally. "Thank you for staying here by my side until he woke up, Sally, but now it's time for you to go see about your man."

"Will you be all right?" Sally asked as she got to her feet, anxious to get back on the trail and go after the men who'd taken her Smoke.

"Of course I will, now that I know Monte is doing all right," Mary said. "Now you and the boys go on and bring Smoke back here safe and sound."

Sally leaned down and gave Mary a hug. "You tell Monte we'll be thinking of him and to get well soon," she said, and then she led the boys out the front door.

"You want us to go get Louis to ride with us, Miss Sally?" Pearlie asked.

She looked up at him. "Of course, Pearlie. Louis would never forgive us if we left him out of this fracas," she answered.

An hour later, they'd picked up their horses at the livery and the four of them were on the trail toward Pueblo, hoping against hope that they were going to be in time to find Smoke alive.

"Hey, men, over here!" Wally Stevens yelled through his cupped hands.

As Cletus and Sarah and the other men rode slowly up to him, they found him standing over the snow-covered dead body of Charlie Blake. Blake was lying on his back with a gaping hole in his throat and frozen blood all around him. Luckily, they'd gotten to him before the scavengers did.

The storm was winding down, and there was even the hint of sunlight peeking through the clouds as the snow disappeared and the wind began to die down. They'd spent an uncomfortable night before the dawn came and they could resume the search for Charlie's body.

Cletus felt a raw knot of anger in his gut. Damn Angus MacDougal and damn Smoke Jensen for this. A good man lay dead whose only fault was trying to help out a friend.

Sarah brushed away tears from her eyes. She didn't want the men to see her crying or to guess the reason. If she hadn't helped Smoke Jensen escape last night, Charlie Blake would still be alive.

Of course, she was intelligent enough to know that Jensen would by now be dead at the hands of her father, but that was only one life. She had a feeling that Jensen was going to cause a lot more deaths before this little trip was over. She wondered what her father would think about that and whether he would consider Johnny's death was worth the deaths of so many other good men.

She grimaced. Of course he would. In Angus's mind, there was no one who was nearly as important as a member of the MacDougal clan. No, she thought with disgust, he wouldn't worry one bit if it cost ten men their lives as long as he got a chance to avenge Johnny's death.

"Pick him up and put him across one of the packhorses," Cletus said.

"And be quick about it!" Billy Free growled, pulling out his six-gun and checking the loads. "That bastard Jensen has to be made to pay for this!"

Sarah looked over at the young man, whose face was flushed and red in the morning light.

"He was only defending himself, Billy," she said in an even tone, glancing from Billy's face to the mountain slopes a couple of miles off in the distance where Jensen had disappeared.

"How can you take his side?" the boy almost screamed. "Charlie Blake was a friend of mine!"

"Charlie was my friend too, Billy," Sarah answered. "And Johnny was my brother and I've got to tell all of you, I'm beginning to wonder if he was worth all this."

The men began to look around at each other, wondering what the hell Sarah was talking about.

"I'm sure Sarah means that she hates to see anyone else get killed because of her taking Jensen prisoner, isn't that right, Sarah?" Cletus said, trying to change her meaning to one the men could understand.

Sarah lowered her head and quickly blinked away the tears in her eyes. "Yes, of course that's what I mean," she said in a firm voice. "I have no sympathy for murderers and gunmen, but I also don't want to put the rest of your lives at risk to avenge the death of one of my family members."

"Don't you worry none, Miss Sarah," Bob Bartlett called. He and Juan Gomez and Billy Free had joined up with the group right after Smoke had ridden off into the storm. "We ain't gonna let no gunslick get away with killin' our friends and neighbors. We ain't gonna stop until we've dragged him outta those mountains feet-first — right, boys?" he yelled, raising his rifle into the air.

The crowd all hollered their assent, and a couple even shot off their weapons into the air.

Lord help us, Cletus thought, looking around at the men as they yelled and hollered. We've gone from a posse to a lynch mob and all it took was one death. I wonder what we'll become after several more of us are killed. Will we still be human, and will we ever be able to forget what's about to happen here in the mountains in the next few days?

"Come on, Clete!" Jason Biggs yelled. "Let's go get that bastard!"

Cletus held up his hands for silence, trying to quiet the mob the men had become. "Listen up, men," he said, keeping his voice level and emotionless. "Take a look at Charlie's body lyin' across that packhorse," he said, inclining his head toward the mount. "You'll notice he ain't wearin' no guns, and if I'm not mistaken, he probably had a long gun or two in his saddle boots on his horse."

"Yeah, so what?" Biggs asked sarcastically. "That just means that son of a bitch Jensen stole 'em."

"What it means," Cletus tried to explain, "is if we go charging up into those mountains, Jensen is gonna pick us off like flies. He's an experienced mountain man who knows what he's doing, and now that we know he's armed with a long gun and a couple of six-killers, we have to be smarter and more careful than we've ever been before or most of us ain't gonna be coming home."

"You sound like you're plumb scared to death of that son of a bitch, Clete," Sam Jackson said, disgust in his voice.

"Respecting the abilities of your enemies ain't being scared, Sam," Cletus answered, not rising to the bait in Jackson's tone, "it's being smart. You want to go hightailing it up into those woods, yelling and screaming and not paying caution no mind, you go right ahead. I'll do my best to find your dead carcass and get it back to your wife so she and your kids can plant you proper."

Cletus's words sobered the men and quieted them down a bit so they weren't so boisterous. "Now, I'm still the leader of this group, an' anybody don't think so is welcome to mosey on along by themselves, but whoever stays is gonna do what I say or I'll put a bullet in their head myself. You all got my drift?" he asked.

There were mumbles of assent, but no one left and no one disputed his right of leadership. "Now, here's what we're gonna do," he said, motioning the men to draw closer so they could hear his plans.

"First off, we're gonna pair up. No one

rides alone or gets out of sight of his partner. Secondly, we're gonna ride with our weapons in our hands, loaded up six and six and the hammer cocked at all times. We're not going to give Jensen a chance to take any more of us out without a fight."

As the men nodded their agreement, he went on with his attack strategy. "Now that the storm has quit, he won't be able to move around the mountain without leaving tracks, so we've got to be careful not to get crosswise with one another and spoil his trail. We're gonna spread out, each pair staying in eye contact with another pair, and we're gonna criss-cross those woods until we pick up his trail, and then we're gonna dog him until we catch him."

"And then we're gonna blow his damn head off!" Billy Free shouted.

Cletus silenced him with a glare. "No, and then we're going to try and capture him, if we can do it without losing any more men," Cletus said. "Angus MacDougal is still paying for this trip and he wants Jensen alive, if at all possible. So, if we can, we're going to try and take him back to the ranch in one piece."

"What if he don't agree to that proposition, Boss?" George Jones asked.

Cletus smiled grimly. "Then we'll blow his ass to hell and back!"

When the men all laughed at this, Cletus said, "Now, let's make a quick camp and get some hot coffee and some good grub into our bellies. It's gonna get awful cold tonight, and I don't want to give our position away by making any campfires. We'll eat a hot meal now, and tonight we'll try and have a cold camp."

"And I want to add another hundred dollars to the man who gets the drop on Jensen so we can capture him," Sarah said.

"What does a man get who puts lead in the son of a bitch?" Billy Free asked sarcastically.

Sarah stared at him. "I'll let my daddy deal with that man," she said, "but I don't think he'll appreciate what my daddy does."

Twenty-five

Smoke had a problem. The storm had stopped and the day was clearing off, clouds disappearing as fast as they'd appeared days before. He knew that with no storm to cover his tracks, the deep snow would lead the gang that had taken him prisoner right to him. Also, his dark clothes were going to stand out against the white snow like a road sign. He was going to have to be very careful moving around to make sure he stayed under cover.

The good news was that he was a good mile and a half up the lower slope of the mountain he'd been heading for. Now the gang was going to have to come after him in his territory, where he was right at home and where they were interlopers.

As he rode, he checked his weapons. He had two pistols, each with six cartridges, and a rather old and beaten-up Winchester that looked as if its owner hadn't cleaned it in years. He shook his head, knowing he wouldn't be able to trust it for accuracy at much over a hundred yards.

He leaned forward, took the canteen off the saddle horn, and pulled its cork, taking a sniff of the contents. He wrinkled his nose. The man he'd killed had had his canteen filled with whiskey instead of water or coffee. That's no good, he thought. His experience had taught him that men who drank whiskey when the weather was below freezing didn't last too long. Instead of warming a body up, as many flatlanders thought, whiskey actually lowered the body's resistance to freezing temperatures.

He guided the horse into the middle of a small copse of trees, so he'd be out of sight from the slopes below, and dismounted. He opened the saddlebags to see what else he'd inherited with the dead man's horse.

Good news at last. The man had a large chunk of bacon wrapped in waxed paper in a sack along with several biscuits and a couple of pieces of jerky. There was also a small can of Arbuckle's coffee, but no pot or skillet to use to cook either the bacon or the coffee in.

No matter, he thought. A good mountain man can always improvise.

In the other saddlebag was an old monocular scope, the kind you pulled out and looked through with one eye. It wasn't as good as a decent pair of binoculars, but it would do. Nestled in the bag was a box of .44 cartridges for the rifle and for the pistols as well. That was an additional fifty rounds he had to add to what was already in the weapons.

In addition to the shells, there was a folded-up yellow rain cape and a small woven blanket and a box of lucifers. Along with the waterproof ground blanket folded behind the saddle, he would at least have some protection against the cold when night fell.

He nodded, grinning. All in all, not too bad, he thought. He had managed to escape and to acquire not only transportation, but also weapons and food and some shelter against the elements. He was ready now to go to war.

He took the telescope and moved to the edge of the copse of trees. He panned the scope all around the downslope area that he could see. There was no sign of any pursuit just yet, which meant he probably had enough time to fix a fire and to eat and make some coffee.

He took the reins of the horse and led it around and through the trees until he found some boulders sitting so there was a small protected space out of the chilly wind on the mountainside.

Using his boot, he scraped the snow down to where the horse could forage enough grass to fill its belly. Unfortunately, the man hadn't carried any grain for his mount, but a few days on grass wouldn't hurt the horse.

He took the saddle and blanket off, and used the reins to fashion a makeshift hobble for the animal, since he didn't know if he could trust it to remain nearby if only ground-reined.

Once his horse was taken care of, he gathered up an armful of dead tree limbs and deadfall from around the boulders. He made a small pile between the boulders, with the smaller sticks on the bottom and the larger ones on top.

He opened the saddlebags and took out the woven blanket. Since the grass around was all covered with snow, it couldn't be used to start the fire. It was too wet. So, he unraveled an inch or so of the blanket, wadded up the yarn, and stuck it under the kindling. When he lit it with a lucifer, it was only moments before he had a small fire going.

He'd picked up only long-dead wood, so there was very little smoke, though there was enough to spot if the men below were looking, and he knew he'd have to make this nooning fast.

He took out the bacon, sliced it with the skinning knife he'd taken from the man's boot, and laid the strips out on a wide, flat rock. This he laid gently in the edge of the fire.

While the bacon was cooking, he poured the contents of the can of Arbuckle's coffee into the sack the bacon and jerky and biscuits had been in, and then he filled the empty can with snow. He placed it near the fire so the snow would melt.

As the bacon cooked and the water began to boil, Smoke dumped a handful of coffee grounds into the water in the can. Using the skinning knife, he cut one of the biscuits open, and then speared the bacon and put it between the halves of the biscuit and began to eat.

The biscuit was very hard, but it softened a bit as the grease from the bacon soaked into it, and soon he could chew it without worrying about breaking a tooth off.

When the coffee was boiling, he wrapped the blanket around his hands and pulled the can away from the fire. He set it down and waited for it to cool down enough so he could drink it.

"All the comforts of home," he mumbled to himself, happy to be free at last.

Thirty minutes later, he kicked snow into the fire to put it out and got back in the saddle. He'd dumped the whiskey out of the canteen after taking a sip or two, and replaced it with hot coffee. He'd also saved some of the biscuit and bacon sandwiches for an evening meal, since he doubted he'd be able to make a fire after darkness came.

He spurred the horse into motion and as it walked up the slope, he glanced behind him. Sure enough, the pine tree limbs he'd tied to the horse's tail were dragging along, smoothing over the prints the horse was making in the snow. It wasn't perfect, and if the men chasing him had a good tracker along, they could still follow him. But to see and follow the tracks, the tracker would have to walk — they couldn't be seen from horseback. This would slow their chase considerably, and for every minute they delayed, the high winds of the High Lonesome were making his tracks that much harder to follow.

He moved farther and farther up the slope, wrapping his blanket around his shoulders as the temperature got colder and colder the higher he went. He glanced upward and smiled to see dense, dark clouds again forming around the distant peaks, whipped around and around by the high winds up on top of the mountain. He knew this meant more early winter storms were on the way, along with temperatures many degrees below zero.

"We'll see how those boys like mountain weather," he said to the back of the horse's head as they slowly ascended toward the snow-covered peaks above them.

Several miles away, Cletus got to his feet as his men finished their noon meal. He moved over next to where the horses were tied and found Jason Biggs standing there, a pair of binoculars to his eyes.

"You see anything, Jason?" he asked as he began to build himself a cigarette.

"Couple'a elk an' a bear, but nothin' that looked like a rider on horseback." He hesitated, and then he added, "I did see what looked like a thin plume of smoke, but with the winds up there it was hard to tell."

Cletus put a match to his cigarette and nodded his head through the smoke. "Yeah, there's just too many trees up there. A hundred men could be ridin' around up there and if they was careful, we wouldn't see nothin' from down here in the flats."

Biggs turned to him. "So, you ready to go upland an' get us a son of a bitch?" he asked, still angry over the death of his friend Charlie Blake.

Cletus nodded. "Yeah, I guess so. I was kind'a hoping Mac would'a been back from talking to Angus, but we can't wait any longer if we want'a get up the side of that mountain 'fore dark."

"Good, 'cause I'm itchin' to get that sumbitch in my sights."

Cletus put his hand on Biggs's shoulder. "Jason, you know we're going up there to capture Jensen, not assassinate him, don't you?"

Biggs showed his teeth, but it was more a grimace than a real smile. "You do what you got to do, Clete, an' I'll do the same."

Cletus decided to let it drop. He too was pretty pissed off about Blake, though he could understand why Jensen had done what he'd done. As he'd told Sarah, a man running for his life will do just about anything he has to in order to survive.

Cletus got his men saddled up and headed toward the steep slopes of the mountain in the distance. Like Smoke, he too noticed the clouds whipping around the peaks, and knew they were going to be in for some rough weather before too long.

When the group came to the trail leading

up into the forest on the side of the slope, Cletus stopped them across the stream from a rotting one-room log cabin that looked like it hadn't been used for years.

"Jimmy," he said, pointing to Jimmy Corbett, "I want you to wait over there by that cabin for Mac Macklin to get here. He'll probably have some more men from Mr. MacDougal, an' I want you to bring 'em on up after us when they get here."

"Yes, sir," Jimmy said, jerking his horse's head to the side and riding toward the shallow, ice-encrusted stream.

"And Jimmy . . ."

"Yeah, Boss?" the boy said, looking back over his shoulder to see what Cletus wanted.

"You'd better fire a couple of shots when you get close to let us know it's you coming." Cletus smiled. "I figure we got more'n a few itchy trigger fingers in this group, and you wouldn't want to sneak up on none of 'em."

Jimmy grinned and touched the brim of his hat as he rode into the stream and over toward the log cabin.

"We gonna sit here all day jawin' or we gonna go up there and git Jensen?" Jason Biggs called from the front of the group of men, where he sat impatiently in his saddle.

Cletus clenched his teeth and walked his horse over next to Biggs's without answering.

He leaned over to put his face close to Biggs's and said in a low voice, "You open your pie-hole like that at me one more time, Jason, an' we're gonna see who the best man with a gun is! You hear me, boy?" he asked, his face red and his voice harsh. His flat, dangerous eyes let Biggs know he wasn't kidding in what he said.

"Uh, I didn't mean nothin' by what I said, Clete, you know that," Biggs answered, his eyes looking down and not meeting Cletus's.

"Remember, Jason, one more time is all it's gonna take. I won't remind you again."

"Yes, sir."

As Cletus rode off, his back turned, Biggs let his hand fall to the butt of his pistol. No one could talk to him like that and get away with it.

Then he looked around at the men gathered nearby. He knew they'd blow him out of the saddle if he shot Cletus, so he relaxed and kicked his horse into following Cletus's. There'd be plenty of time later for Clete to have an accident.

Twenty-six

Sheriff Wally Tupper handed the dally rope he had attached to the two pack animals behind him to Jack Dogget, one of the men riding with Angus MacDougal.

"Here's your dynamite and gunpowder and extra shells, Angus," he said, trying as hard as he could to keep his anger out of his voice.

Angus MacDougal tipped his head. "Come on with us, Wally," he said, though this time it was more in the way of an offer instead of an order. "I promise you it's gonna be fun. After all, hunting a man is much more exciting than hunting elk or bear, and I'm offering a bonus of five hundred dollars to the man who catches that son of a bitch."

Wally shook his head. "No, thanks, Angus. I think I'll stay here."

Angus stared at him, his eyes narrowing. "I get the feeling you don't think much of what I'm doing, Wally. Am I right?"

Wally nodded. "Yep, you're right as rain, Angus. I told you, Jensen ain't done nothing wrong — leastways nothing against the law. Everybody there that day says he fired in self-defense — that Johnny prodded him and drew on him without any provocation."

"Bullshit!" Angus screamed, making his horse stomp and crow hop a time or two. "He killed my boy, and he's going to pay for it!" Angus's face was beet red and his eyes were wide and full of madness. He looked like he was about to have a stroke.

Wally shook his head sadly. "Maybe he did kill him, Angus, but Johnny wasn't no boy. He was a growed man who shot his mouth off and got himself killed for drawing on the wrong man at the wrong time. It was bound to happen sooner or later, and if it hadn't have been Jensen, it would've been somebody else."

"You saying my boy deserved to get killed, Wally?" Angus asked, his voice suddenly low and dangerous but the madness still in his eyes.

Wally sat up straighter in the saddle, tired of being a whipping boy for this crazy old man. "Yeah, I guess that's what I am saying, Angus, and it's long past time someone told you like it is."

Angus smiled grimly. "This is a dangerous time to try and grow a backbone, Wally."

"Maybe, Angus, but I'll tell you this straight. If you go up in those mountains and kill Jensen, that's your business 'cause it's out of my jurisdiction. But if you bring him back here and do it, then I'll see that you hang for it."

"Those are awfully big words, Sheriff," Angus said, looking around at the twelve men sitting on their horses with him. "I hope you can back them up."

Wally looked around at the men, his face paling just a bit. "These men all agreed to go out with you to catch a gunman, Angus. I don't think they agreed to kill an officer of the law."

Angus snorted through his nose. "Well, we'll just have to see about that when I get back."

Wally nodded. "Things are going to be different when you get back, Angus. That's what you'd better be thinking on while you're up in those mountains."

Angus growled and spurred his horse right at Wally, waiting for him to jump out of the way. But Wally stood his ground, and it was Angus who had to pull his horse to the side and ride off toward the mountains in the distance.

Wally sat watching him as he rode off with his hired gunmen. He felt sorry for the old man, but his day was dead and gone, like his son. From now on, Wally intended to be a sheriff for all of the people of Pueblo, not just the MacDougals. And if they didn't like it, then they could just lump it.

As they rode up the mountain slope past the log cabin at its base, Cletus followed the tracks of a lone horse in the knee-deep snow.

"Spread out, men," he hollered. "Ride in pairs, but keep within sight of the pairs on either side of you and keep your hands on your guns. If Jensen fires on us, everyone take off after him."

As his men spread out, Sarah stayed next to Cletus, riding as his partner. He rode slowly, flicking his eyes from the tracks in the snow in front of him to the mountainside up ahead of him, trying to see if there was any movement up there where a man might be lying in wait.

He felt the sweat start to ooze out of his pores and freeze on his forehead, and the hand that was holding his pistol developed a slight tremor. Damn, he'd never been afraid of a man before, and he'd gone up against some of the meanest men in the West in his day. Maybe he was just getting old — too old to go traipsing through the woods after a man who'd saved Sarah's life only a couple of days before.

Sarah saw the sweat glistening on Cletus's face, and felt ashamed of the situation she'd put him in by bringing Jensen up here and then setting him loose. Cletus had been like a father to her for more years than she cared to remember. In fact, he'd been more of a father to her than her real dad. Angus had always had eyes only for Johnny, and he'd made it clear that he was going to leave the ranch to him, not her.

Sarah tried to think of some way to get them all out of this mess, get the men to give up and go on home. But for the life of her she couldn't think of anything to say that would make them give up the hunt. They were all too afraid of Angus MacDougal. They knew if they returned to the ranch without Jensen, Angus would make their lives miserable, or he'd kill them. The old man wouldn't like his orders being disobeyed, especially when they concerned the man who'd killed his favorite child.

She could only hope that Jensen would keep right on riding and they'd never find him. If he stayed and fought and more men were killed, more men like Charlie

Blake who were friends of hers, she didn't know if she could live with herself for what she'd done.

As they rode, she offered a silent prayer that Jensen would never be seen or heard from again.

Up ahead, Smoke had used his time to good advantage. He'd explored the area of the mountainside, and now he knew his way around as well as if he'd lived there for years. As he rode around exploring and learning the various trails, he spent his time preparing traps and deadfalls to bedevil his enemies.

Sharpened stakes were set in shallow holes along the trail, and then snow was thrown over them to hide them. Heavy branches were pulled back and tied to rope along the ground so they'd release and knock men off their horses when they were on narrow trails next to cliffs and ledges. He'd found and remembered where there were large boulders that could be pushed down the mountain to start landslides in case the men following him got too close.

He was ready for war. He wondered if the men riding up the hill after him knew what they were getting into. He doubted they did, or they would've turned tail and ridden away as fast as they could.

Cletus slowed and held up his hand when he saw a man's footprints next to the horse's in the snow. Evidently Jensen had dismounted here for some reason.

Signaling the men on either side of him to circle around in front, he got off his horse and walked it slowly along toward a thick copse of trees up ahead, his pistol out and the hammer cocked.

When he entered the grove of trees, he found the boulders and the remains of Jensen's campfire. He knelt and felt the coals. They were still warm, but not hot. Jensen had been gone from this place a while now.

Cletus holstered his gun, but signaled Sarah to keep hers out. He walked around the camp and searched the ground on all sides of the copse of trees. That was strange, he thought. There were tracks coming into the grove of trees, but none leaving it.

He stood there, looking around, scratching his head. Damn! The man couldn't just fly out of here without leaving any traces, could he?

He glanced up at the sky as the sun suddenly darkened. Heavy, black clouds were whirling around the sky, and the temperature was dropping while the chilly north wind was picking up. A storm, and a big one from the feel of it, was definitely coming soon.

He stood there thinking. Jensen only had two ways to go. He could go up, or he could've circled around and be heading back down the mountain on their flanks.

For his money, he felt Jensen would go higher. Jensen was an old mountain man, this was his playground, and he wasn't about to give up his advantage by heading for the flatlands. No, Cletus knew Jensen was up above them somewhere, and he was probably looking down at them at this very moment.

Well, the hell with him, Cletus thought, getting angry. Sarah had given the man a chance to get away clean. If he chose to stay and fight, then Cletus planned to give him a fight he wouldn't soon forget. And he surely didn't intend for any more friends of his to get killed in the doing of it.

He swung back up into his saddle and waved his men forward and upward.

Twenty-seven

Smoke was indeed watching the group as Cletus's men weaved in and out of the forest on their way higher up onto the mountainside.

"Time to sow a little hate and dissent," he mumbled to himself as he took the telescope from his eye and picked up the old Winchester he'd stolen.

Instinctively he aimed a little lower than it looked like he should, since he was shooting downhill. He was a good three hundred yards up the hill and was well hidden, lying on his stomach behind a ponderosa pine that'd been felled by lightning. He'd stacked snow on the brim of his hat so the only thing visible from below would be his dark eyes. Not much of a risk since his targets were so far away.

He put the bead on the end of the rifle barrel about three inches above the head of one of the men far off to the right, and slowly squeezed the trigger. He didn't expect to hit the man, but he hoped the rifle was accurate enough to at least come close enough to scare the man.

The rifle exploded and kicked back against his shoulder. Smoke immediately pulled the gun back to him and lowered his head a couple of inches. He knew it'd take the sound of the gunshot a second or two to reach the men below, after the bullet had already landed.

The man Smoke had aimed at screamed at the top of his lungs and pitched sideways off his horse. Suddenly, most of the men below were firing their pistols and rifles in all directions as the sound of Smoke's gunshot echoed and re-echoed around the mountainside, distorting the direction from which it had actually come.

The man Smoke knew as Cletus rode rapidly over to the wounded man, lying low along his mount's neck to make himself less of a target.

As soon as Cletus got to the man, he jumped off his horse and held his hands up in the air, hollering, "Stop shooting! Cease firing!" as loud as he could.

The gang's shooting slowed and finally stopped, but it was clear to Smoke from the way the men turned their heads back and forth that they were frightened. It was also clear that most of these men weren't gunslicks or hired guns, but merely cowboys who were out of their depth in this kind of fracas.

When the men had stopped their firing, Cletus told the ones nearby to keep a sharp lookout and he bent down over Billy Free, who was lying in the snow, holding his right arm with his left hand and moaning and groaning as he writhed on the ground.

Cletus said, "Hold on, Billy. Let me take a look at where you got hit."

Free moaned again, but moved his left hand. Cletus saw a hole in Free's right arm just below the shoulder that was leaking blood slowly. A good sign that no major artery had been hit.

Cletus raised the arm, causing Free to clamp his jaws together and to almost shout out in pain. The bullet had gone through the arm, and was sticking in the heavy leather of Free's fur-lined winter coat.

Cletus took Billy's bandanna from around the boy's neck and wrapped the arm tight enough to stop the bleeding, making Billy groan again. "Good news, Billy," Cletus said. "The bullet went right on through and the bone ain't broken. You should do all right if'n it don't get infected."

"Did anybody see where the bastard fired from?" Billy asked as he struggled to sit up in the snow.

Cletus shook his head. "No. Evidently, he was far enough away that nobody saw the muzzle flash nor heard the report until he'd ducked back in hiding."

Suddenly, there was a loud thumping sound followed immediately by the sharp report of a rifle shot, and Wally Stevens's horse screamed and reared up before collapsing onto a shouting Wally.

Wally hollered as loud as he could for somebody to get his damn horse off his leg.

"I . . . think it's broken," he sobbed, grimacing and holding his right thigh with both hands.

George Jones and Sam Jackson jumped off their horses, and struggled to lift Wally's horse enough for him to slide his leg out.

Sure enough, the leg just below the knee was bent at an unnatural angle. Luckily, there was no bone sticking out, but the leg was going to have to be set, and it was a sure thing that Wally was not going to like that, nor the long ride back to the ranch on horseback.

Cletus waved his arms. "You men get off

your horses and take cover behind trees," he shouted. "And for God's sake, see if you can spot where the gunshots are coming from."

The men complied with Cletus's order, and soon all of them were hugging trees in a wide semicircle, their eyes pointed up the hill as they looked for any sign of Jensen.

Up above, Smoke smiled and eased back away from the tree trunk he was behind. Now, he had all the men that were after him sitting around watching for him. As the temperature dropped they'd get colder and colder since they weren't able to move around. Just what he wanted, and they wouldn't dare gather around a fire because it would make them perfect targets.

He grinned as he eased up into his saddle and walked his horse over a ridge and away from the men below. Now, he had to find a good spot to make a fire so that when darkness fell, he'd be able to heat some coffee and finish off the last of his bacon and jerky and get some of the chill out of his bones.

An hour later, after Wally's leg had been set and a couple of tree limbs used as a splint, Cletus looked around at his men. They were all shivering and slapping their arms against their chests as they hid behind trees looking for any sign of movement up above them.

It suddenly dawned on Cletus what Jensen was up to. The sly son of a bitch wanted his men half-frozen to death and scared to move.

Damn, he thought. He got to his feet, feeling an itchy sensation in the back of his neck as he imagined the mountain man drawing a bead on him. "Come on, men," he shouted, waving them to their feet. "It's gonna be dark 'fore long an' we gotta find a place to make camp."

Bob Bartlett, whose face was red and chapped from the cold, stammered out, "It's gonna get colder'n a well-digger's belt buckle tonight, Clete."

"Yeah," Carl Jacoby agreed, looking up at the darkening sky, which was full of dark roiling clouds. "And it looks like more snow's on the way too."

"Exactly," Cletus agreed. "That's why we've got to find a place we can defend that's protected from above so we can make a fire and get warm."

"I ain't sittin' next to no fire an' makin' myself an easy target," Sam Jackson said grimly.

Cletus shrugged. "Good, Sam. Then

when morning comes we'll throw your frozen carcass on the coals to thaw you out so you can sit a saddle."

By the time darkness had fallen, Cletus had managed to find a series of large boulders that were lying in a line across the slope of the hillside. He had his men make a camp on the downhill side where they'd be safe from gunshots from above, and he built a large fire.

"Clete," Sarah said when she saw the pile of brush and limbs he'd stacked up. "Jensen will be able to see that fire for miles."

He shrugged and grinned. "You think he don't already know exactly where we are, Missy?"

"Uh . . . I guess he does at that," she agreed.

"Now, I'm gonna build this here fire and get some hot vittles into the men, 'cause if'n I don't, they're gonna freeze to death. But while we're eating, I'm going to have some sentries out so that Jensen won't be able to sneak up on us or take any potshots at us."

"You think sentries will stop him?" Sarah asked.

"Probably not, but I think Jensen's

gonna be doing just what we're doing to-night. Trying to stay outta the storm and get some heat into his body. I don't care how long he was a mountain man. That don't keep his blood from freezing just like anybody else's."

When she nodded, he slapped her on the back. "Now, get on over there and help the men get some coffee made and some beans and fatback cooked up so's we can eat."

"Yes, sir, Mr. Cletus, sir," she said, snapping off in insolent half salute and grinning as she turned and moved over to the pack-horse that carried their supplies.

They'd just finished eating when a gun-shot came from down the hill, followed quickly by a shout, "Yo, the camp!"

The men sitting around the fire all jumped to their feet, their pistols in their hands and worried looks on their faces as Cletus shouted, "Put those guns away, men. That's Mac Macklin's voice."

Moments later, Angus MacDougal and the men with him rode slowly into the light of the campfire. Daniel Macklin was riding at MacDougal's side.

"Damn, Clete," Angus said as he dismounted and walked over to stand near the fire with both his hands outstretched in front of him. "That fire feels good. I'm froze clear down to the bone."

Clete looked over at Juan Gomez. "Juanito, would you boys cook up some more beans and fatback and put some more coffee on to boil. Looks like we got company for supper.

"How'd you find us in the dark?" Cletus asked Angus.

"Hell, boy, you can see this fire for five miles," Angus answered. He looked around at how Cletus had arranged the fire behind the boulders so his men were protected from above.

He nodded in approval. "Right smart move, Clete, making your camp here."

Cletus smiled and turned to pour himself some coffee from the pot. Guess the old man's forgotten all the times we camped out surrounded by hostile Indians in the old days, he thought.

Twenty-eight

As they sat by the fire next to each other, Angus told Cletus that he was taking over the hunt for Jensen.

"You're welcome to it, Angus," Cletus said, relieved that he wouldn't be in charge any longer. "I got no more stomach for this anyway."

"What do you mean by that?" Angus asked around a mouthful of bacon and beans.

Cletus drank his coffee, staring over the rim at the fire without looking at Angus. "I just don't think Jensen is the killer you make him out to be, Angus."

Angus swallowed his food. He couldn't believe what he was hearing. "You mean you don't believe he killed my Johnny?" he asked.

Cletus turned to look at him. "No, I know he killed Johnny, Boss. It's just that I think Johnny probably didn't give him no choice in the matter, that's all."

"Bullshit!" Angus growled. "He shot my boy down in cold blood."

Cletus shook his head. "First off, Angus, Johnny weren't no boy, he was a full-growed man, though I got to admit he often didn't act like it."

Angus glared at Cletus, hate in his eyes at this desecration of his son's memory.

Cletus went on. "Not only that, but on the ride back here, after Sarah betrayed him and took him prisoner, Jensen risked his own life to save hers."

Angus opened his eyes wide in disbelief. "What?"

Cletus told him the story of Smoke and the rattlesnake and how he'd thrown himself in front of Sarah.

Angus clamped his jaws shut. "That don't make no never mind. Fact is, he killed Johnny and for that he's gonna die, no matter what he did for Sarah."

From the other side of Angus, Sarah interjected, "Daddy, I think you ought to listen to Clete. He's right about Jensen. He isn't a cold-blooded killer like you say."

Angus's face twisted up in hatred and he swung a backhand, slapping Sarah across the face.

"Don't you dare say nothing against your brother, girl," he snarled. "He was worth two of you."

As Sarah's hand went to her face, Cletus

reached across Angus and grabbed his wrist, twisting hard until Angus groaned in pain. "That tears it, Angus. I'm through with you and your little gang of killers. And if I ever hear of you laying another hand on Sarah" — Cletus paused and looked over at her — "I'll personally come out there and beat the living shit out of you!"

Cletus got to his feet and helped Sarah to hers. He put a palm against the side of her face, his eyes sad. "I'm sorry, Missy."

She glanced from Cletus back down to her father. "Me too, Clete. Come on. Let's get out of here."

The two walked over to the string of horses and began to saddle their mounts.

"You leave me now, Clete, and you'll never work in Colorado again!" Angus shouted at their backs.

As Cletus and Sarah swung up into their saddles, Cletus shook his head at the old man. "I wouldn't make threats you ain't gonna be able to carry out, Angus. For my money, I don't think you got one chance in ten of riding off this mountain alive."

"And just where do you think you're going, young lady?" Angus growled at Sarah.

She sat up straight in her saddle. "I'm

311

going home to pack my things. It's about time I left home and made my own way in the world."

"Well," Angus snorted, "good riddance to the both of you. You'll both come crawling back to me when you realize I'm right about all this."

Cletus shook his head. "No, Angus, we won't be back. And I don't think you've been right about anything for a very long time."

They jerked their reins and rode off alongside one another without looking back, leaving Angus staring after them as the darkness swallowed them up.

Smoke heard this exchange from where he stood in the darkness less than a dozen yards away. It had been no trouble for him to sneak near the camp, moving between the sentries as silent as a ghost in the pitch-black night. He could have snuck up to any of them and killed them before they knew what was happening, but he wanted to end this with as little loss of life as he could. There'd already been too much killing.

The knee-deep snow helped to cover any sounds he might make, but would show his tracks later in the morning light. He smiled to himself, unworried about that. He planned to give the men in the gang plenty of other things to be thinking about before the sun rose in the morning.

Moving slowly and staying out of the light of the campfire, Smoke snuck over to the string of horses where they were tethered along a rope stretched between two trees. He walked along the broncs, his hands lightly touching their rumps so they wouldn't get nervous and whinny, until he came to the pack animals. Their packs had been removed and sat on the ground next to them, and he was lucky the men hadn't bothered to take the boxes of supplies and ammunition and explosives up near the fire where they would have been safe.

It took Smoke five trips to carry all of the boxes of dynamite and gunpowder and extra cartridges a couple of hundred yards away from the camp. He needed them to be that far away for what he had planned. On his last trip, he used his clasp knife to cut the rope holding the horses, but made no effort to scatter them. That would come later.

When he was far enough away, he opened the boxes and took out fifteen or twenty of the sticks of dynamite, along with their fuses and detonators, and stuck them in a saddlebag. He then took a fuse, cut it two feet long, and stuck it and a detonator into a stick of dynamite. He took a can of gunpowder and, using his skinning knife, he opened the top, wincing at the scraping sound the knife made.

He set the can between the boxes of dynamite and gunpowder and cartridges and put the stick of dynamite in it, nestling it down into the powder. He struck a match and lit the fuse, and then ran as fast as he could around the edge of the camp until he was on the opposite side from where he'd set the supplies.

While he waited for the fuse, he took out one of the sticks of dynamite from his saddlebag and stuck a detonator and a very short two-inch fuse into the end of it.

Three minutes later, the dynamite and gunpowder and cartridges all went up with a tremendous bang. The fireball from the explosion rose fifty feet in the air, and set the top of one of the ponderosa pines on fire.

The force of the explosion blew men off their feet and tossed them about like rag dolls, causing several to suffer broken arms and lacerations from flying debris.

The extra cartridges in the pack were set off by the blast, and bullets flew through the air like a swarm of angry hornets, wounding two men. The rest of the gang threw themselves on the ground with their hands over their heads while they screamed in fright and terror as slugs whined past their ears.

Smoke kept his head down until things had quieted down. Men slowly got to their feet, shaking their heads and pulling their pistols from their holsters as they moved off in the direction of the explosion.

Suddenly, Daniel Macklin shouted, "Hey, Mr. MacDougal, the horses are all gone!"

Angus got to his feet and brushed himself off, his ears ringing and his nose running from all the dust and dirt in the air.

"Well, just don't stand there, men. Round 'em up!" he shouted, pointing with both hands as horses ran around in the forest, as frightened as the men were.

Once all of the men had stumbled out of the camp and out into the woods looking for horses, Smoke leaned over the boulder he was hiding behind and pitched his stick of dynamite into the campfire.

He'd managed to run only a dozen yards when the dynamite went off, exploding in the campfire and blowing what was left of the camp into smithereens.

At least half of the men's saddles were

destroyed, along with most of their sleeping blankets and ground covers. All of the rest of the food supplies were ruined, with the exception of several cans of Arbuckle's coffee, which were smashed and dented but remained somehow intact.

As the bedraggled group of cowboys and gunslicks limped their way back into what was left of their camp, a light snow started to fall.

Angus gritted his teeth and glared at the skies above. "This is perfect," he growled, "just perfect!"

By the time morning came, Angus's men had managed to find about three quarters of the horses, and the injured and wounded had been patched up as best they could with what supplies they had remaining.

Another campfire had been built, and the men breakfasted on coffee made with melted snow. There wasn't any food left that was worth eating.

The snow continued to fall, but at least the wind was not too strong, and the temperature actually seemed a bit warmer than it had been the night before.

All in all, the men counted themselves lucky there'd been no loss of life in the explosions of the night before.

Twenty-nine

As the bedraggled group of men sat around the campfire drinking their coffee, Angus got to his feet. "I'm not gonna let that bastard Smoke Jensen get away with making Angus MacDougal look like a fool," he said in a loud voice.

Off to one side, George Jones whispered to Sam Jackson, "Don't seem to me like the old man got much choice. The deed's done been done."

Angus glared at the men for interrupting his speech, though he couldn't hear what they'd said. "As I started to say, Jensen ain't gonna get away with this. I'm offering five hundred dollars to the man what puts a bullet in Jensen."

Carl Jacoby glanced at Mac Macklin, sitting next to him. He shook his head and stood up. "But Mr. MacDougal, that makes us no better'n bounty hunters."

"So what, Jacoby?" Angus asked belligerently. "You got a problem with that?"

"Yeah, I do," Jacoby answered. "Me and most of the boys here signed on to help you get Jensen 'cause we knew he'd killed your boy and thought he deserved to be punished." He paused. "Now a lot of us ain't all that certain of the facts of what happened in Pueblo last year, and we damn sure didn't sign on as hired killers."

Angus's face turned beet red and he shouted, "You keep your mouth shut, Jacoby, or you'll be fired."

Jacoby shrugged. "That's all right, Mr. MacDougal. I don't think I want to work for you any more anyway." He turned to the group of men sitting around the fire. "I don't know about the rest of you, but Mac Macklin and me, along with Sarah MacDougal and Cletus Jones, all think Jensen wasn't at fault for killing Johnny MacDougal. Now maybe that don't matter to some of you, but I ain't gonna hunt down and kill a man what don't deserve it, no matter how much money Angus offers." He turned back to Angus. "I quit."

"Go on, you coward!" Angus shouted. "None of the rest of the men are going with you."

"I don't know about that, Mr. Mac-Dougal," Macklin said as he got to his feet. "I ain't no bounty hunter, and I sure as hell ain't no killer neither. Wait up, Carl, I'm coming along too."

Slowly, almost all of the men around the campfire got to their feet and made their way over to the few remaining horses, some looking at MacDougal with disgust, others with pity, but none looking afraid of him as they used to be.

Jacoby looked back over his shoulder. "We'll take the buckboard for the injured men and try and double up on the mounts so we can leave you enough to get back to the ranch on," he said as they began to hitch up a couple of horses to the wagon and put blankets on the backs of a few others.

By the time the men had all gone, Angus realized he only had four men staying with him. Jason Biggs and Juan Gomez from his ranch, and Jack Dogget and Joshua Stone from the group that Wally Tupper had gotten from town.

He nodded and rubbed his hands in front of the fire to get them warm. "You men won't regret staying," he said, his eyes gleaming with madness. "I'm gonna make you rich."

After the men and Angus had gathered up as much ammunition as they could find that hadn't been destroyed, they climbed up on their horses and began to follow the tracks Smoke had left when he bombed the camp.

Angus was in the lead, riding up a narrow trail that skirted the edge of a precipice along the side of the mountain. He could look to the side and see a drop of four hundred feet over the side.

Suddenly, his horse stumbled, its legs falling into the hole Smoke had filled with sharpened stakes. The horse screamed in pain as the wooden stakes pierced its legs, and it bucked and jumped to the side, falling off the cliff.

Luckily, Angus had been thrown from the saddle, and fell on the edge of the cliff, his arms wrapped around a cluster of small pine trees and holding on for dear life. Dogget and Stone jumped off their mounts and pulled Angus up and over the edge until he was standing on firm ground.

Angus looked down into the hole and saw the stakes, slapping his thigh and cursing. "That tricky son of a bitch!"

Dogget and Stone got back on their horses and walked them around the hole and up the trail, ignoring Angus standing there.

As Biggs and Gomez rode by, Biggs leaned over and offered his hand. Angus took it and swung up on the horse's back behind him. "Don't you worry none, Mr. MacDougal," Biggs drawled. "We'll get that bastard for you."

Angus nodded, but he was beginning to have his doubts. So far, Jensen seemed much smarter than the men he'd hired to go after him.

Maybe it hadn't been such a good idea for him to come up here and lead the group himself.

Thirty minutes later, as they continued to follow Jensen's tracks in the snow of the trail along the edge of the cliff, going slow so as not to fall into any more holes, Jack Dogget's horse tripped a rope stretched across the trail and hidden just under the snow. As the rope was tripped, it let go of a large branch that had been pulled back and tied in place. The branch whipped forward, catching Dogget full in the chest. The force of the blow slammed him backward off his horse and over the cliff in an instant.

The men riding behind him barely had time to blink before he was out of sight, and all they could hear was his screams as he fell four hundred feet to his death.

"Sweet Mary Mother of God!" Juan Gomez whispered, crossing himself as his face broke out in a heavy sweat. "Jensen is *el Diablo!*"

"What'd you say, Juan?" Angus asked.

"He said Jensen is the devil," Biggs answered, his eyes wide, "and I don't know as what but I agree with him."

Suddenly, from up ahead, Gomez whispered, "Madre de Dios!"

"Now what are you saying?" Angus asked, until he saw where Juan was staring.

Up ahead, standing in the middle of the trail, was a man dressed in buckskins. He had a pistol in a holster tied down low on his right leg, and another pistol stuck in his belt facing his left hand. He was standing in the trail as cool and composed as if he were out for a walk.

"Jensen!" Angus hissed as he looked over Biggs's shoulder at the man.

"That's right, Mr. MacDougal. Now that the odds are fair, I'm ready to face you and your men head-on."

"Odds fair?" Josh Stone asked incredulously. "But it's four to one."

Smoke shrugged. "That's about right, I 'spect. I want to give you men at least a fighting chance."

"Holy shit!" Biggs whispered.

"Now, you can hook and draw, or you can turn tail and ride on off and live to enjoy another beautiful day in the High Lonesome," Smoke said, seemingly unconcerned about their decision. "It's your choice."

"Son of a bitch!" Stone yelled and went for his gun, as did Biggs and Gomez.

Angus had never seen anything like it. One minute Jensen was standing there, as cool as a cucumber; the next his eyes were on fire and his hands were full of iron and he was blazing away at them.

Stone was hit in the throat, the slug blowing out the back of his neck and almost decapitating him. His body fell to the side, the head flopping back and forth on a slender thread of tissue.

Gomez didn't even clear leather before he was hit twice, once in the left chest and the other bullet hitting him right between the eyes, blowing the back of his head off and leaving a cloud of red mist hanging in the air as Angus and Biggs were showered with bits of skull and brains.

Biggs actually managed to get his gun out and cocked before Jensen's fourth slug took him in the gut, bending him over with a loud grunt. The fifth shot entered the top of his head and stopped his groaning as if a switch had been turned off.

As Biggs's body fell off the horse to land

facedown in the snow, Angus stuck his hands straight up in the air, his face a frightened mask of terror.

"I've got one bullet left, Mr. Mac-Dougal," Smoke said calmly, seemingly unaffected by his killing of three men in less time than it takes to tell it. "You want to try your luck?"

Angus shook his head violently from side to side. "Uh, no, please don't shoot me," he cried, tears running down his cheeks.

"You're a pathetic excuse for a man, MacDougal," Smoke said, holstering his pistol as he walked toward the broken man. "Your son was an asshole, but at least he fought his own battles. He didn't hire other men to do his dirty work for him."

Angus held his hands out in front of him like he was warding off an evil spirit as Smoke walked up to him.

Smoke reached up, took Angus's gun from its holster, and threw it over the cliff. He leaned to the side and spit into the snow, as if he were getting rid of a bad taste in his mouth.

"You'd better go on home, MacDougal. To what home you have left, that is," Smoke said, his voice filled with disgust as he turned and walked away.

Thirty

Sally and the men riding with her, Louis, Cal, and Pearlie, finally reached Pueblo after a hard few days' ride. They'd encountered no resistance along the way, which surprised Louis but not Sally.

"There's no reason for them to be watching their back trail, Louis," she'd said when he remarked on the absence of any sentries or guards. "They've already got Smoke where they want him, or he is already dead."

Louis had looked at her, his mouth open, his eyes sad.

She'd smiled grimly at him. "Oh, don't think I don't know that is a possibility, Louis, old friend," she'd said, her eyes blazing. "I hope to find him well and alive, but if I don't, I will survive it." She'd hesitated, her face set. "I will survive it, but the men who carried this out will not."

As they rode into town, Louis said, "I think we ought to start with the sheriff. He's bound to know this Sarah Johnson and where her parents live."

They rode up to the sheriff's office, and all got down off their horses and walked through the door.

A rotund man of average stature was sitting behind his desk, his feet up on one corner, drinking coffee when they entered. Upon seeing Sally, the man jumped to his feet, grinning his most engaging smile.

"Howdy, ma'am, my name's Wally Tupper. I'm sheriff of Pueblo. How can I be of assistance to you?"

"Hello, Sheriff Tupper," Sally said, equally engaging. "My name is Sally Jensen. I'm from the town of Big Rock and I'm looking for a young woman named Sarah Johnson."

They all saw the blood drain from Tupper's face as his smile faded like a snowflake on a hot stove. "Uh, I don't know any Sarah Johnson, Mrs. Jensen," he said, his voice croaking on the words.

Louis stepped forward. "Maybe her name's not Sarah Johnson, Sheriff," he said. "She's about this high, attractive, with long brown hair, and is in her mid-twenties. You know anyone fits that description around here?"

"Uh . . . no. Why are you looking for this woman?" the sheriff asked, sweat appearing on his forehead.

Louis cocked his head. "Why would you need to know that if you don't know anyone by that description, Sheriff?" Louis asked, his eyes boring into Tupper's.

"I guess . . . I guess I don't," the sheriff answered weakly.

Sally said, "Come on, men, let's go ask around town."

Louis set his hat on his head and glared at the sheriff. "Tell you what, Tupper," he said in a low dangerous voice. "We're going to make our way around town asking everyone we meet about this girl. If I find out she lives here and you lied to us, I'm going to come back here and have another talk with you — and I promise you won't like the results."

As Sally put her hand on the door, the sheriff wiped his face with a handkerchief and flopped into his desk chair. "There's no need for that," he said in a defeated voice.

Sally turned back around. "Sheriff, I believe this woman has something to do with the kidnapping of my husband. I think she and her friends mean him harm, so you had better tell us what you know or I will have the U.S. marshals down here to see just what part you played in all this."

Tupper nodded slowly. "You are right,

Mrs. Jensen," he said. "The woman you describe is named Sarah MacDougal, daughter of Angus MacDougal. About six months ago, your husband was here with these gentlemen and shot and killed a young man named Johnny MacDougal." He sighed and wiped his face again. "I do believe the MacDougals are interested in revenging that death by killing your husband."

Louis stepped forward. "Sheriff, you know from your investigation that Johnny MacDougal started that fight and was killed in self-defense. Didn't you tell the MacDougals that?"

Tupper nodded. "Yes, I did, but they wouldn't believe me. Old Angus, and now his daughter Sarah, has been on the warpath for Smoke Jensen ever since the shooting. None of them will listen to reason."

"But Mr. Tupper," Sally interrupted. "You are the sheriff of this county. Why didn't you do something to stop them from attacking my husband?"

Tupper held out his hands. "You don't understand, Mrs. Jensen. Angus Mac-Dougal owns the biggest spread in these parts and is a very powerful man. You just don't go up against him if you want to keep your job."

Louis snarled and reached over and jerked the tin star off Tupper's chest, ripping a large hole in his shirt. He contemptuously tossed the star in the wastebasket next to Tupper's desk. "You don't deserve to wear that badge, Tupper. You were elected to represent all of the people and uphold all of the laws, not just those agreed to by the rich and powerful."

Tupper hung his head, his face flaming scarlet. "I know, don't you think I know that? I thought I had the guts to stand up to Angus. But I guess I'm not the man I thought I was."

"Where is this MacDougal ranch, Mr. Tupper?" Sally asked. "And what is the fastest way to get there?"

At that moment, Smoke was riding up to the MacDougal spread, his shoulders slumped with fatigue.

He had pushed his horse as hard as he could, taking a shortcut over the mountains to get to the MacDougal ranch before any of the hands could arrive. He knew the approximate location from the talk he'd heard around the campfire when he'd been prisoner.

He rode directly up to the barn and got down off his horse. Working as fast as he could, he got two horses out of the corral next to the barn and hitched them up to a wagon.

He drove the wagon over to the ranch house and pulled it to a halt. Stepping down, he walked up on the porch and knocked on the door.

An elderly lady answered the door, and looked at him with startled eyes. "Yes, may I help you?" she asked.

Smoke took off his hat and held it in front of him. "Are you Mrs. MacDougal?" he asked politely.

The woman straightened up and looked over at him regally, as if she were royalty. "Yes, I am. My husband and I own this ranch. As I said before, what can I do for you?"

"Is anyone else in the house?" Smoke asked, glancing over her shoulders.

"Sir, that is certainly no business of yours," Mrs. MacDougal said haughtily.

Behind her, Smoke could see the Mexican housekeeper appear in the kitchen door.

With a sigh, Smoke pulled his six-gun and said, "I'm sorry to disturb you, ladies, but I'm going to have to ask you to come out of the house."

"Oh, my God!" Mrs. MacDougal almost

screamed, her hands going to her face. "He's going to kill us!"

Smoke sighed and shook his head. "No, I'm not, Mrs. MacDougal. I'm just going to send you away from here for a while."

As the two women filed out of the front door, glancing apprehensively over their shoulders at Smoke, he waved them out to the buckboard and helped them climb up onto the seat.

"Can either of you drive one of these?" he asked.

"I can, young man," the housekeeper said.

"Good," Smoke said, handing her the reins. As soon as she had them in her hands, he whacked the nearest horse on the rump and the wagon took off, both women screaming in terror.

Smoke walked back to the barn, got a can of kerosene and some rags, and made his way back to the house.

Sally and Louis and Cal and Pearlie rode as fast as they could down the road toward the MacDougal ranch, hoping they would get there in time to save Smoke's life.

Sheriff Tupper had finally broken down and told them of the twenty or so men Angus had out in the mountains going after Smoke. Sally and her friends hoped to find someone at the ranch who could show them which of the many mountains surrounding Pueblo was the one where the hunt was taking place.

As they rounded a corner, they were almost run down by a buckboard racing down the trail toward town. They jerked their horses' reins and barely got off the trail in time.

Pearlie scratched his head at the sight of two women in the racing wagon, both of whom were still screaming at the top of their lungs as the buckboard careened down the road.

"You think I should go and try and help them?" Cal asked Sally.

She shook her head. "No, they'll be all right. This is a smooth trail and shouldn't give them any problems. We need to get to the ranch and see if we can find Smoke."

Less than an hour later, they rode up to the ridge overlooking the MacDougal spread, and were astonished to see the main ranch house and the barn engulfed in flames.

"Holy smoke!" Cal whispered as the four sat on their horses staring at the burning ranch.

A voice called from a nearby clump of boulders as a head appeared on top of the largest rock. "You folks looking for me?"

They turned their eyes and saw Smoke sitting on top of the boulder watching the ranch burn.

Sally jumped down off her horse and ran as fast as she could toward her husband, who'd also jumped down off the rock and was running toward her.

After they'd embraced and kissed — and kissed some more, Sally leaned her head back and said, "And just what is going on here, Smoke Jensen?"

He looked down at the burning buildings. "I'm just teaching a man a lesson, sweetheart. He lost his son, through no fault of his own, but then he went out seeking vengeance, and now he's lost his daughter, his best friend, and his home. I only hope the lesson sticks."

He put his arm around her and walked her back toward their horses. "Now, let's go home," he said, a smile on his face. "I don't believe I was quite through welcoming you back home when I was forced to leave."

Author's Note

I've done a lot of things in my life, most of which I can't talk about, but when I began writing, I knew I had found my niche in life. I have written more than a hundred books, and am well into my second hundred. I like to hear from my readers. You can write to me c/o the publisher, or e-mail me at dogcia@aol.com

The employees of Thorndike Press hope you have enjoyed this Large Print book. All our Thorndike and Wheeler Large Print titles are designed for easy reading, and all our books are made to last. Other Thorndike Press Large Print books are available at your library, through selected bookstores, or directly from us.

For information about titles, please call:

(800) 223-1244

or visit our Web site at:

www.gale.com/thorndike
www.gale.com/wheeler

To share your comments, please write:

Publisher
Thorndike Press
295 Kennedy Memorial Drive
Waterville, ME   04901

336